This series is dedicated to my late father, William Harold Clutterbuck, himself a railwayman. In giving his son a Hornby train in 1937, he passed on a bug which still claims me firmly. My only regret is that he is no longer with us to see the results. Thank you Dad, for all you did for us.

STEAMING

INTO THE

HEYDAY

Tales of the Great Western Railway at its Zenith

Michael Clutterbuck

HEDDON PUBLISHING

www.heddonpublishing.com
www.facebook.com/heddonpublishing
@PublishHeddon

Introduction

The period between the World Wars can be classified, certainly in the UK, as the heyday of steam. By 1938 Gresley's A4 managed 125 mph down Stoke Bank with a light train, becoming the world's fastest steam locomotive (although Germany's 05002 made 124.5 mph on almost level track and with a regular train), and then showing films and offering haircuts to passengers between London and Edinburgh. Stanier in the LMS was producing the first of his magnificent Pacifics; Maunsell of the Southern had built the Schools – the most powerful 4-4-0s in Europe, and the GWR had claimed the world's fastest train, the *Cheltenham Flyer*. The four big railway companies were hoping to achieve even greater things when war intervened and their service to the country imposed such burdens on them that they never had any real chance of recovery before the government nationalised them and they ceased to exist.

The Great Western Railway was a private transport company which served the west of England and most of Wales with distinction for over 100 years until it was taken over by the government, along with the other three main railway companies, in 1948. During those years, the company proved itself to be very competent at supplying the transport needs of the travelling public, and in doing so engendered a remarkable degree of loyalty among its staff. Once, in the mid 1970s, an Australian teaching colleague returning from his first UK visit asked me what was so special about the GWR that people were still talking about it in Bristol 30 years after it had ceased to exist. Aside from the years of government control during the world wars, the GWR was unusual among the big four in that it paid a dividend every year, even during the financially troubled early 1930s.

What *was* special about the GWR? It had its own way of doing things and appeared to have been able to attract men of real ability: Messrs I.K. Brunel, D. Gooch and G.J. Churchward are three examples on the engineering side, but Sir Felix Pole in management was also partly responsible for the greatness of the Great Western. Indeed, many people today (myself included) still have fond memories of the Brunswick green locomotives and the brown-and-cream carriages they recall from their youth. The coverage of the West Country holiday areas no doubt had an important bearing on such memories. As a small boy during the Second World War, I clearly recall standing in my father's allotment a mere five yards away from the unfenced main line between Chester and Birkenhead, watching entranced as the trains hurried by, although by that time during the war they were no longer as bright and clean as my Hornby trains.

The level of interest in the GWR still puzzles those who know little of Britain's railways during the years of private ownership. Fortunately, aspects of the GWR can still be experienced in a number of tourist railways: visitors to The Great Western Society's centre at Didcot, to 'Steam', the huge museum in Swindon, or even to the tourist railways at Bridgnorth or Llangollen can still see and even experience what it meant to travel by 'God's Wonderful Railway' in the heyday of steam.

I note with interest that a 'Great Western Railway' has indeed re-appeared in the UK.

Mike Clutterbuck, Melbourne 2016

The lines featured in *Steaming into the Heyday*

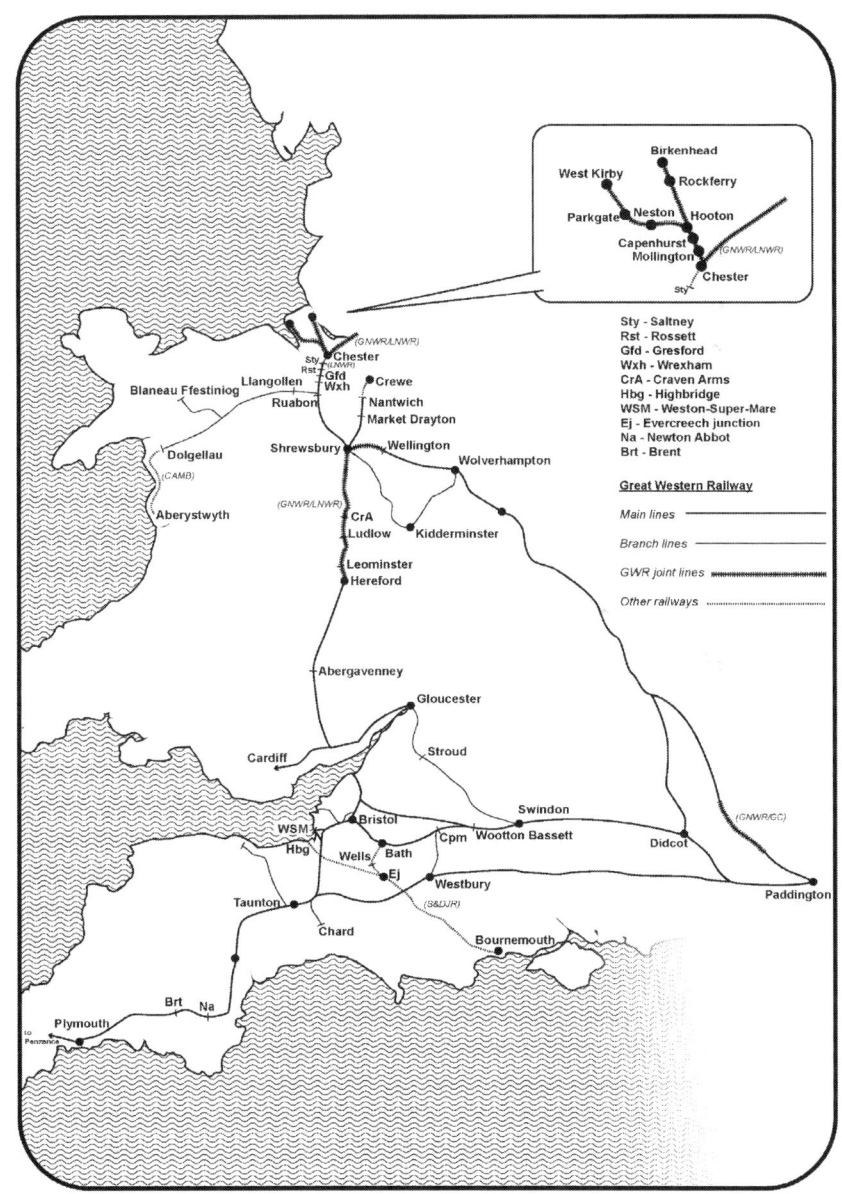

Steaming into the Heyday

Tales of the Great Western Railway at its Zenith

1 - Young George comes to a decision (1897 - 1900)

The country, it seemed, was awash with flags and bunting. Wherever one turned, celebratory messages were strung over even the meanest of streets as the nation celebrated the 60th year of Victoria's reign. There was indeed much to celebrate: Great Britain was by far the most powerful nation in the world, with its vast empire and industrial might. Its navy ruled the waves and even the army was showing embryonic intelligence. Gone were the days when a moneyed but half-witted aristocrat could buy a whole regiment and destroy it through sheer incompetence (the Crimean War had been won largely because their French allies had been rather better organised and the Russian army was even more incompetent). Some senior army officers had even recognised that bright red uniforms turned soldiers into excellent targets and had proposed khaki uniforms for offensive purposes. There were limits, however; although the Indians and Sudanese had been firmly taught to respect their 'betters', the Boers had been bullied sufficiently to show that a tiny but determined group could make a serious nuisance of themselves and were about to make a laughing stock of a British army which had still not fully understood that intelligence and military ability among its senior officers was a useful requirement. The Germans were flexing their muscles, having defeated the Danes, the Austrians and the French in short order 30 years earlier, and their technological and engineering achievements were assisting them to create their own empire. The Americans, too, were gradually realising their enormous industrial potential.

But such thoughts did not occupy the mind of Henry Denton, a Great Western Railway driver of Westbury (Wilts) shed who was walking with his nine-year-old son George; the driver to the station and the boy to school. They stopped to admire an army band marching past with drums beating and bugles sounding proud martial airs. The boy gazed, entranced, at the soldiers in their dress uniforms, many bearing medals.

Henry looked as his son stared at the soldiers and smiled. "The army for you, lad, is it?"

Young George nodded his head. "I think so, Dad; Freddy Braithwaite's dad is a sergeant in the army and he says it's a good life as a soldier."

Henry nodded, "He could be right, too. So, you're thinking of becoming a soldier?"

George paused, "Yes, but I like trains, too."

"Did you know they have engine drivers in the army?"

George stared at his dad in surprise; "They do?"

"Of course, they have a lot of engineers in the army. I have even heard talk of them building their own railway to train engineers."

"You mean I could be a soldier *and* an engine driver?"

"Ah-" Henry hesitated; the boy was a bit too smart, "I'm not sure I'd go quite that far. Let's wait and see. You're only nine and you have to concentrate on your studies at school."

But immediately in his mind, young George could see himself as a soldier in the thick of battle: *The natives with their bows and arrows, spears and occasional guns were yelling as they attacked. A company of his regiment was cut off nearby and was running out of ammunition. The driver of their narrow gauge military supply train was lying on the little footplate, a spear through his chest. Brave Sergeant George Denton raced over to the train, pushed the driver to one side, and drove the train, dodging spears and arrows hurtling into the cab as he heroically brought the desperate men their boxes of ammo. After the battle the general smiled as he awarded a medal to...*

"Morning Henry," the greeting by the ticket inspector as they passed through the barrier at Westbury station came as a sharp interruption to the boy's reverie, "and hello to you, young George." He let them through onto the platform without demanding to see tickets.

They waited for a few minutes to see an express pull in, hauled by one of William Dean's beautiful 'Single' engines, gleaming in its Brunswick green with Indian red frame and wheel centres, and all set off with polished brass fittings. The brown-and-cream clerestory coaches merely added to the splendid vision as the train drew slowly to a stop. Henry nodded in appreciation as the driver of the express brought his train smoothly to a halt. He walked over to the engine to see who the driver and fireman were.

"Morning, Isaac," George's dad called, "good run so far?"

The driver came over to see who was addressing him. "Oh, morning to you too, Henry; yes, can't complain, she's running nicely."

His fireman glanced back down the platform as the two drivers were chatting. "We've got the green, Mr Jacobson," he said as the guard's whistle sounded.

Driver Jacobson gave a quick wave as he returned to his side of the cab and took hold of the regulator lever. A moment or two later, the train began to move gently, and Henry and young George watched it glide out of the station, on into the distance, bound for Plymouth.

"Have you ever driven one of those engines, Dad?" George asked.

"Oh yes, often," said his father, "they can certainly run fast with a light train, but with today's heavier trains it's not so easy. I preferred to drive them seven or eight years ago when we still had the broad gauge; not only did they look good, they were fast."

Five years previously, the Great Western Railway had finally abandoned its last stretch of Brunel's seven-foot gauge, which it had introduced on its inception in 1835. Most of the other railways at the time had opted for Stephenson's gauge of four-foot-eight-and-a-half inches; this division had caused no end of transfer problems when goods and passengers had needed to be transhipped wherever there was a change of gauge. The Gauge Commissioners had, after some debate, concluded that although the broader gauge had undoubted technical advantages, these were outweighed by the huge costs which would have been incurred in converting the majority of railways to the seven-foot loading gauge. The Great Western had gradually converted its route mileage to the standard gauge. But the loyalty of drivers for the broad gauge had been very strong; indeed, one old engine driver who had been run over by a locomotive muttered as he lay dying, "At least it warn't one o' they narrer gauge injins."

George was thoughtful on the walk to school as he left his father at Westbury shed; he was quiet in the classroom and only answered questions when asked directly. His Latin teacher was puzzled; George was usually a pupil who could be relied on to take an active part in the class.

"Anything wrong, young Denton?"

"Er- no, sir."

"You're very quiet today."

"Just thinking about what I want to do when I grow up, sir."

"And what is that, pray?"

"I want to be an engine driver, sir."

The teacher nodded, "A laudable ambition, Denton."

"Yes, sir."

"Good; now I am convinced that an accurate knowledge of the Latin nouns of the second declension will enhance your later skills on the railway. Consequently, I should value your undivided attention for the rest of the lesson."

"Sir."

At home, later that day, his parents were equally puzzled, unaccustomed to their son's silence.

"Anything wrong, son?" Henry wanted to know.

"No, Dad, I've just been thinking about what I want to do when I grow up."

"I see, and have you decided to go soldiering?"

"No, I don't think the army has engines like the express engine we saw today. I want to drive engines like you do."

"Hmmm," said Henry. "I hope you are not saying that just because it's what I do. You must make up your own mind."

"I've always liked trains, you know that, but seeing that big engine today made me think I'd like to do that one day."

Henry shook his head. "You'll be disappointed, George. It takes many years to learn to drive engines, and by the time you are ready those Singles will all have gone. They might be good-looking engines but modern express trains are getting too heavy for them."

"How long does it take to learn to drive?"

"It varies; first you have to start as a cleaner, then after a few years if the boss trusts you, you might be allowed to fire an engine in the yard. You could then become what we call a Passed Cleaner, which means you can act as a fireman with an experienced driver. If you show some ability you might proceed to qualified Fireman. The next step involves passing driving exams to become a Passed Fireman; this allows you to drive under supervision until you have sufficient experience to become a Driver. After that it's a question of moving up in the links to the top duties, usually driving the express passenger trains."

"How long does all that take?"

"Depends on your interest, ability and dedication. It often takes twenty or thirty years to become a driver. You have to be patient, and-" Henry warned, "some firemen never become drivers."

"When could I start?"

"The Great Western will take you at the age of fourteen."

After George had gone to bed, Henry Denton reported the conversation to his wife, who shook her head. "No need to worry – he's got another five years to think about it."

"I think he's serious about this, Martha; you should have seen his face when that train came in."

"He could do a lot worse, Henry; the job's made you pretty happy so far."

"Yes, but it's been a long, tough road."

"You've managed, so why shouldn't George?"

"I was hoping for an easier life for him."

"You've worked hard all your life, Henry, but you are an engine driver for the GWR; that's a rewarding job which is also widely respected these days. Why shouldn't George have the same?"

Henry had no answer to this, and in any case, the question was rhetorical.

Over the next three years, Henry tried to interest his son in a variety of possible jobs, including engineering with the army. While George showed a willingness to understand what his father was doing for him, it made no difference to his basic ambition to join the railway.

The matter was finally concluded on the boy's twelfth birthday. When he came to breakfast, the table had been pushed to one side and there on the floor was a circle of track, and a little Bassett-Lowke model steam locomotive with two carriages was waiting to be fired up and set to run. Martha and Henry had given up; they knew there was no longer any chance of their son changing his mind. George hardly touched his breakfast and quickly picked up the engine to try and work out how to fire it up. Fortunately, it was a Saturday and his mother allowed him to miss out on some of his chores so he could get to grips with running his very own railway.

Over the weekend, Henry and his son spent many happy hours with the model train.

"What's this 'GBN' on the engine for, Dad?"

"It stands for 'Gebrüder Bing Nürnberg' - the manufacturer. Germans make many trains for the Bassett-Lowke model railway company."

"Why don't we make our own trains?"

"I expect we will, one day. Now, playing with your train is all very well, but have you finished your homework?"

"Oh Dad, you always ask that!"

"Yes, because like today, you always try to dodge the question."

Young George sighed; sometimes it was really hard being a child. He couldn't wait to grow up.

2 - George becomes a railwayman (June 1902)

The letter directed George Denton to present himself at Swindon Works at 8.00am the following Wednesday, with a signed note of recommendation from his headmaster. It was accompanied by a voucher for a Westbury-Swindon return fare.

On the appointed day, George got up very early. He was at the station in plenty of time to catch the train to Chippenham where he had to change for Swindon. At Swindon Works, the procedure began with a medical test in which George had, amongst other things, to suffer the indignity of an intimate all-over examination. This was followed by a request to sort a large range of strands of wool into their different colours, in order to check his eyesight for colour blindness - an immediate cause for failure for potential engine drivers.

The later interview was equally thorough, but George's father had prepared him well and he had no difficulty in fielding the questions asked. The interviewer finally nodded in satisfaction and George was told to report to the shed foreman, sometimes known as the shedmaster, at Taunton on the first of the following month at 7.00 am; digs would be arranged for him.

George's first week at Taunton was somewhat trying; he was required to make the tea for the older apprentice cleaners and act as a general dogsbody, doing all sorts of jobs which were beneath the dignity of those lofty enough to have been in the company for several months. The week brought a further indignity to him as he was initiated into the cleaning gang; a ritual whereby four larger lads took him into the toilet, lowered his trousers and proceeded to 'clean' (as they put it) him with a rag soaked in heavy engine oil. He was only partly mollified by being informed that all apprentices went through the same trial, and most took it in good part after their initial, understandable, anger.

George later decided that in spite of tradition, he didn't want to put up with another such indignity as part of his initiation, no matter what the other apprentices were prepared to accept. Unfortunately, as he was shorter than most his age, his refusal to undergo any further ritual was not considered relevant. He took particularly strong exception to his tea being doctored with a dose of cod liver oil. The three lads who held him down so they could pour the mixture into his mouth succeeded merely in pouring the liquid over his chin and face. They discovered that, small though he was, he could hold his own, and the ensuing damage to their faces, clothes and the room led to all four being hauled up before their charge-hand, who was not amused. Thereafter, the other apprentices tended to leave him alone, but this was a two-edged sword: although no more tricks were played on him, neither was he accepted into the group for several months. Apart from his obstinacy, George showed, in the minds of too many other cleaners, two other faults: he was conscientious in his duties, and he was smart. While these characteristics impressed the charge-hand, they did not endear him to those apprentices of a more indolent nature. It brought to the attention of the overseer one or two of their little dodges, which consequently lost their value. Revenge was sought but it proved ineffective as George took little notice of the minor irritations which came his way.

On one occasion, however, even George's patience was sorely tried; at a lunch break when several apprentice cleaners were sitting round a brass casing which had been removed for attention to the safety valves, George lifted his lunchbox out of his bag to enjoy the sandwiches his landlady had cut for him.

"What on earth-?" he exclaimed. The sandwiches in his lunchbox were coated with soot.

He stared around. "Who did this?" He bunched his fists, his face white with anger. There was no reply.

"Come on, which of you gutless wonders ruined my lunch with soot?"

Nobody, it appeared, wanted an interview with the foreman.

Sam Huddlestone stood up. "I'll tell you one thing, Denton," he said as he strode away, "it warn't me."

Ben Mitchell spoke up, addressing the whole group; "I'm all for having a laugh and pulling the leg of a new lad," he said, "but ruining a bloke's lunch is not funny." He turned to George, "Here, Denton, share my lunch with me."

"Thanks, Mitchell," said George, "I'll remember this." He took the proffered sandwich.

The mood among the group was subdued after that and they went back to work, cleaning the Pannier tank engine they had started on that morning.

The following week, George was in the cab of an elderly 4-4-0 Duke class engine, polishing some of the levers which had acquired a touch of rust, when he heard two apprentices talking quietly on the ground next to the locomotive. They had sat down and were drinking their mugs of tea.

"You should 'ave seen 'is face!" Sam Huddlestone's voice was unmistakable, "'e would 'a gone 'ungry too, if that stupid Mitchell 'adn't've shared 'is lunch wiv 'im. Mind you, I was a bit worried 'e might 'ave known it were me and tried to smack me about. I would've belted 'im back ter last week, but we would've both 'ad ter see the foreman, 'an if I 'ad ter see *'im* a third time I'd get the sack fer sure."

George smiled and crept silently down the steps on the other side of the cab, waiting until he saw Huddlestone and his friend walking away. He climbed back into the cab and continued cleaning the rust off the levers. *Right, Sam Huddlestone, I'll have you for that!* he thought with satisfaction.

The next day, George brought a bar of chocolate with him and sat down with the other cleaners; he opened his sandwiches and put the bar of chocolate down near Sam Huddlestone. He then got up quickly and said, "I must go to the lav before I eat." He left quickly and when he came back, the chocolate was gone.

"Anyone seen my chocolate?" he asked. "I thought I left it here."

"Yer not lookin' at me, I 'ope," said Sam Huddlestone loudly. George noticed a slight brown smear near Sam's lip.

"No; I must have left it somewhere else. No matter."

The group continued chatting and eating until Sam Huddlestone dropped his sandwich, paled, and abruptly jumped up. "Christ! I've got ter go ter th-" He raced off in the direction of the toilets.

"What's got into Sam?" said one lad, puzzled.

"Looks like he was running off to the bog," said another.

Ben Mitchell looked at George. "It was you, Denton, wasn't it?" he said with a grin, "What was in that chocolate?"

"Laxative."

Hoots of laughter followed and thereafter, the apprentices decided that fooling with Cleaner Denton tended to backfire, and they wisely left him alone.

Management had found George lodgings with a local widow, whose husband had been killed in South Africa. She was an elderly lady with two grown-up children and she treated her new charge with a degree of kindness, not to mention fine cooking. George's digs were two miles from the shed and the daily walk in all weathers was useful in getting him accustomed to his later work in the cabs of older locomotives built when enginemen were expected to be a hardy breed; there were still plenty of engines in service with either only half a roof to their cabs, or none at all. George was able to get home once every two months for a weekend, although the Great Western Railway was not inclined to reimburse him the fare; this made a further dent in his meagre wages.

Nevertheless, he was happy enough in his work and, as an attentive learner, rapidly won the respect of some of the regular engine crews who specifically requested him on the cleaning gang preparing an engine for an express duty. They had learned that he would not be satisfied with anything less than a perfect shine on the cab and boiler.

He quickly familiarised himself with the myriad other duties about the steam shed, apart from just cleaning the engines. Able to squeeze into the firebox, he learned to assist in replacing any broken fire bars or bricks from the brick arch. There was ash to be shovelled from the ash pits into wagons and fitters' tools to be carried to and from engines which needed attention. On the locomotives themselves there was plenty to do: sand had to be filled into locomotives' sandboxes; ashpans needed cleaning. A stationary boiler – lifted from the frames of an engine marked for scrapping - was used for heating and drying the sand to allow it to flow easily from the sandboxes onto the track, assisting the adhesion of the rail. This boiler had to be lit, coaled and fired, just as it had been in its mobile life, though without the complications brought about by rough track, gradients, and the need for constant attention. There were magic moments when a passed fireman or driver would allow George to stay in the cab while they were moving an engine about the shed yard, although he was not permitted to touch the controls.

Over the succeeding six years, George gained in experience necessary for the range of duties he was required to perform. He was particularly interested in locomotive handling, and he learned that coupling rods linked the driving wheels, and that connecting rods linked these to the cylinders. He found out that cotter pins were for enabling fine adjustments to the big ends; he was surprised to find that the driving wheels were actually sprung in order to allow for irregularities in the track and so the coupling rods had to be jointed.

George gradually acquired a reputation for having an instinctive feel for life in a locomotive cab and one morning, when he was walking into the shed to take up his cleaning duties, the driver of the Minehead 4-4-2T tank engine waiting to set out for its train at the station, leaned out of his cab. "Hey up, young Denton; hop up into the cab with us, you're needed here."

George obediently climbed into the cab, "What's the matter, Mr Simmonds?"

"My fireman here is not feeling too good and I've had permission to grab a cleaner to take with us to help out if need be. You're it."

George was delighted. Cab experience for a cleaner, especially out on the road, was seen as a sign of great trust, and could lead to advancement. But Driver Simmonds did not allow George to just sit and observe; he was required to do a great deal of firing, although there didn't seem to be anything much wrong with Fireman Gifford, who sat and watched with a smirk on his face.

On his return to Taunton shed, George was very tired but elated at the day's work. According to his driver he had proved more than capable of handling the duty and thereafter was occasionally used for similar local runs. In short, life for Cleaner Denton was developing in a very satisfactory manner.

3 – Passed Cleaner Denton (November 1908)

There was a distinct mood of optimism among GWR employees, something of the pride that had been missing since the final demise of the broad gauge in 1892. One of the main reasons for the new spirit of elation was the series of new and powerful engines emerging from Swindon Works. Mr Dean's engines of the preceding century had shown an elegance second to none in the country, but Mr Churchward, who had taken over as Chief Mechanical Engineer after Mr Dean's retirement and death, had begun to produce some remarkable locomotives. He studied French and American designs and was perfectly prepared to adopt what he thought was valuable from both camps. He had even imported three 4-4-2 French engines for evaluation and had modified them to suit GWR conditions as well as building some comparable engines GWR-style, which he trialled against the French machines to identify superior features that could be usefully incorporated into his later designs. The result of his research and experiments was paying handsome dividends: fast and powerful two-cylinder Saint class 4-6-0s, and four-cylinder Star class 4-6-0s express locomotives were emerging from Swindon works and taking over the heavier duties, enabling increased speeds with accompanying reductions in journey times.

Rumours abounded in Taunton shed and management had – in vain - tried to put a stop to them. Four years previously, one of the City class 4-4-0s - *City of Truro* - was said to have taken an Ocean Mails express down Wellington bank at 100 miles per hour. It was no secret that these express passenger engines, with their six-foot-eight driving wheels - were fast, but no British steam engine had ever been formally recorded as doing a tonne anywhere (although a German electric train had managed 123 mph near Berlin). The Great Western had been trying to outdo the London and South Western with mail and passenger trains from the west to London, just as the LNWR and Caledonian had tried to outdo the Great Northern, North Eastern and North British railways from London to Aberdeen ten years earlier. But this 'Race to the North', as the newspapers had dubbed it, had also been stopped before any serious accidents could happen. In Taunton shed it was widely believed that the footplatemen on the *City of Truro* had been threatened with instant dismissal from the company if they made any public mention of their achievement and so questions at the pub, artfully plied by journalists during the consumption of alcoholic beverages, had been equally artfully deflected.

George had continued to impress his colleagues, as well as management, at Taunton with his handling of firing trips to Minehead and, increasingly, to other local destinations. He was now finding himself on a firing turn with a senior driver on a fairly regular basis, whenever regular firemen reported sick. This practice remained highly unofficial but the management with a blind eye recognised it as a useful solution, especially as it did not incur any extra cost; George remained a cleaner and was still paid accordingly. George himself had no objection because he saw this as all adding to his footplate experience. Admittedly, his cab work was restricted to tank engines and the smaller tender engines, but he was getting to know most of the drivers and they were, in general, only too glad to help and advise him.

One week there had been a serious flu outbreak at Bristol's Bath Road shed and a number of cleaners from other nearby sheds had been brought in to help out. George had been included and he spent a week working on Mr Churchward's large Star class passenger locomotives; engines they didn't often see in Taunton shed, although they passed through the mainline station in common with the Saint class 4-6-0s, frequently on the West of England expresses. George noticed that many of the Stars were now seen as 4-6-0s rather than as the 4-4-2s of their original construction.

He once found himself cleaning one of the three sophisticated French locomotives and his urge to move up the promotion ladder was getting stronger, in line with the rising reputation of GWR engines since Mr Churchward had taken the reins.

One early afternoon at the end of the week in Bristol, George was standing with Bill Hollingworth, a Taunton driver, on the platform at Bristol's Temple Meads station, waiting to catch a train back to their shed.

"Crikey, I'm cold!" muttered Driver Hollingworth to George with a shiver.

"Cold?" replied George taken aback, "It's warm today!"

"Well, warm or not, I'm bloody freezing!"

Their conversation stopped when a Plymouth express drew in. As the big Star pulled to a halt, the fireman leaned out of the cab.

"Hey! You two railwaymen?"

"Yes," called Driver Hollingworth, "why?"

"I need a replacement driver, my mate's taken ill!"

Driver Hollingworth climbed into the cab, followed by George. "What's wrong with your mate?" he asked.

"Dunno, he just can't stand without getting dizzy all the time."

"Sounds bad; you're right, he'll have to be replaced. Look, I'm a driver; I can take your train on, and I know the road to Plymouth. We can drop Cleaner Denton here off at Taunton on the way."

"That'd be a great help, we might even be able to keep time, but we'll have to get Bert seen to."

After the sick driver was escorted off the engine and Control informed of the change of crew, the express moved off with only seven minutes lost. They gradually picked up speed as Bill Henderson eased the regulator upwards.

"I'm Passed Fireman Dan Murphy, by the way," said the fireman of the express, "of Laira shed."

"A Plymouth man," nodded Bill Hollingworth, "you'll be glad to get home. When did your driver become ill?"

"Just after we left Bath."

"You must have had a nasty few minutes, then, on your own in the cab. Good job you're a Passed-" Bill swayed and grabbed the side of the cab with his left hand.

"What's up?" asked Fireman Murphy nervously, "you alright?"

"I think so, I just had a bit of a turn."

But when Driver Hollingworth had a second 'turn', Dan Murphy said to George, "Here, lad, grab my shovel and see what you can do while I have a look at your driver."

It was clear that Bill Hollingworth was also unwell and could not continue, so Dan took over the regulator while George tried firing. He had often fired before and knew the rudiments, but had never handled the shovel on a big express locomotive, let alone at any speed; nevertheless, he kept the fire burning sufficiently for the driver's use. He was even working the injectors to add water to the boiler, under the occasional approving gaze of Bill Henderson, who was resting on the fireman's perch and warming himself whenever the fire-door was open.

"We'll be losing time again at Taunton when you and the lad get off, Driver Hollingworth," said Dan Murphy sadly. "I was hoping we could make it all the way to Plymouth."

"We won't lose any time in Taunton, Passed Fireman Murphy," said Bill Hollingworth. "I'm well enough to keep an eye on young Denton here, so if you can keep driving, we'll make Plymouth yet."

"But I have to leave in Taunton!" George was worried at what his shedmaster might say.

"When?" asked Driver Hollingworth.

"I'm supposed to go back to Taunton shed today, sir."

"Well, so you will; you'll just go via Plymouth. But of course, if you feel you're not up to it, then-"

George paused in his shovelling and stared back at the Taunton driver; "I'm up to it!"

Yet George soon discovered that his firing experience of little tank engines with six coaches on stopping trains to Minehead or Chard was not the same as firing a Star on an express with twelve on. The big firebox of the Star required a great deal of coal, not to mention carefully placed shovelling; by the time they had reached Exeter, George was streaming with sweat and blisters were beginning to form on his hands.

At Exeter St David's, he had a few minutes to relax, but his mood was not lightened by Bill Hollingworth: "Not bad, Cleaner Denton, not bad at all; but that was the easy bit," he winked at Dan Murphy; "it's the coming Devon Banks which show what real firemen are made of."

Passed Fireman Murphy added his two bob; "Yes, I'm a Passed Fireman and even I have to sweat to fire my train up Dainton Bank and through Brent."

Leaving Exeter, George was seriously worried – would he make it or would he have to ask for help across South Devon? He was nervous as they swept down towards Newton Abbot, but as they drew up at the platform there was a Bulldog 4-4-0 locomotive standing next to them on the through line, ready to act as a pilot engine.

"See what we've done for you, young Denton?" said Bill Hollingworth. "We knew you would have difficulty over South Devon, so we called ahead for a pilot engine to assist you."

On the one hand, George was relieved to see the pilot back onto their train but, equally, slightly disappointed that, after his strenuous efforts, the other two didn't seem to think he could manage; he wasn't even going to be given the chance to prove his mettle. Dan Murphy slipped out to change the headlamps while the fireman of the pilot put the two express headlamps on the buffer beam of his own engine.

The run over the South Devon banks showed George that any fireman would have his work cut out to manage a train to Plymouth, and he was exceedingly glad to have the assistance of the pilot engine; he would certainly have disgraced himself without it. The steep gradients were, Bill Hollingworth told him, a result of Isambard Kingdom Brunel's original plan to have this section of the line worked by the atmospheric system, whereby the trains (far lighter in those days, of course) were drawn by the vacuum in front of a cylinder in a large tube placed between the rails. The system had not been successful and was quickly abandoned.

With the three men working well as a team, the express drew into Plymouth on time and they received vocal appreciation of their achievement from the platform staff at Plymouth.

One week later, George was delighted to hear that his name had been put forward for the Fireman's exam; this had been done, the shedmaster told him, on the strong recommendation of Driver Hollingworth, as well as his own Charge-hand Cleaner.

George passed the exam and was promoted to Passed Cleaner with firing duties as and when needed. In spite of his pleasure at the promotion, he privately admitted to the shedmaster that he had not been able to fire the Star on his own over the Devon banks.

"Fire an express on your own over South Devon?"

"No, sir," George bowed his head in shame, "they had to organise a pilot engine for me."

The shedmaster guffawed at this. "They did no such thing; they were pulling your leg! Most heavy expresses have a pilot waiting for them at Newton Abbot as routine; any fireman would struggle without one!"

4 - George fulfils an ambition and gets a shock (October 1910)

Over the preceding eight years, life had served George Denton well, and he had been both entertained and able to develop his firing skills to such an extent that he had reached the position of Fireman from Passed Cleaner at a relatively early age. His father was delighted and his mother nodded wisely; she was also proud of her son's achievement and hoped that he would have the same satisfaction in his career that her husband enjoyed.

Already, George was known to be ambitious and prepared to take on any jobs; even those that other firemen were reluctant to tackle. He felt that such jobs would give him valuable experience in dealing with a range of situations which footplatemen could expect in the course of their daily work. These included adapting to the widely varied needs of heavy, unfitted freights, including frequent starts and stops for signals and lay-by sidings, and in particular undertaking extra duties upon entering long downhill gradients when the driver had to devote all his attention to easing the train at the start. It was vital for the engine crew and guard to understand each other's needs and co-operate well if they were to maintain tight control over their train.

Unfitted trains had controlled brakes only on the locomotive and guard's van; the brakes on the vans and wagons could only be applied when the train was at a standstill or moving slowly enough for the fireman to run alongside and unhitch the handles in passing and then heave the brake levers down to lock them on. On the approach to a downhill run, it was sometimes necessary to stop the train and apply the brakes on the vehicles before proceeding. The inertial weight of a heavy freight could, under some circumstances, push a locomotive, even with its brakes full on, downhill and out of control. On the rare occasions when this happened, the only course for the locomotive crew was to abandon the train by jumping from the cab and hoping that nothing was ahead until it came to a standstill.

Passenger trains had continuous braking - vacuum brakes on all vehicles which could be applied from the locomotive, thus making them far easier to manage on downhill runs. Yet passenger trains, particularly expresses, were usually much faster, and this produced a different set of problems, especially if the driver missed a signal. The Great Western, in its search for increased safety, had introduced an automatic train control system, whereby a short ramp was set between the running rails at a distant signal and, if the signal showed 'caution', a shoe under the locomotive was lifted by the ramp, causing a warning siren to sound in the cab. The driver, on hearing the warning, could cancel it and apply the brakes in time to bring the train to a stand at the next signal. If, however, the driver failed to heed the warning within a set time, the brakes were automatically applied, bringing the train to a stop. The system was proving to be very effective and a boon to drivers, who welcomed it. It was gradually being extended over the GWR network.

Fireman Denton was gradually increasing his own familiarity with the signals and hazards on an increasing number of routes, all of which made him an asset in his shed. A wide route knowledge was also a great advantage in terms of prospects of promotion. He was already familiar with firing most of the smaller locomotives that Taunton shed was responsible for. However, aside from the run with that big 4-6-0 Star class over the South Devon banks, he had not fired any of the larger express engines and he was eager to try.

One morning in early September, George found himself scheduled to fire a semi-fast from Plymouth to Swindon. The Plymouth men were to crew the train to Taunton, where George and his driver would take it on to Swindon. As the train entered Taunton station, George couldn't believe his eyes.

"It's a Single!" he called in delight. "I've never fired one of these."

"So what?" Larry Kemp was clearly unimpressed; "what's so special about the Dean Singles? They're almost twenty years old, they're old-fashioned, and they don't like heavy trains."

"But they're such beautiful engines!" George's enthusiasm was hardly dampened by Larry's lack of it.

"They're also going to scrap or rebuilding," his driver's comment was like a cold shower.

"Scrap?"

"Or re-boilering," Larry said; "a few of them are getting newer, modern boilers, but I suspect that's only temporary – they'll all be gone soon."

"But why?"

"Because we've got far better engines now, that's why."

Their 4-2-2 locomotive was, in fact, going to Swindon for modification, including re-boilering; the parallel boiler was to be replaced by a more modern tapered boiler, although many wondered whether the work was actually worth it, as several of the class had already gone to the scrapyard. In truth, there were far better engines arriving from Swindon Works under the aegis of Mr Churchward; but for intermediate duties, the picture was different: the draconian bean counters in head office imposed strict limits on the number of new engines each year. The only way the Locomotive Department could meet greatly increasing demands from the Traffic Department (and the travelling public) was to rebuild older, successful classes with bigger and more efficient boilers, to achieve greater power.

The powerful Star and Saint class 4-6-0s were appearing in greater numbers and were proving to be masters of all the crack expresses the GWR could give them. Indeed, there had recently been an exchange with the LNWR: one of the new Star 4-6-0s had been loaned to the LNWR for trial on their main line from Euston to the north, in exchange for a latest LNWR Experiment class 4-6-0 to run from Paddington. The Star had shown itself to be vastly superior to LNWR 4-6-0s, whereas the Experiment had not impressed the GWR at all. Some had wondered why the LNWR hadn't sent one of its new George V class 4-4-0s which were meeting with approval; they were probably unaware that the new CME, Bowen Cooke, had resorted to the only means he knew to get modern, powerful engines on to LNWR metals – making the Premier Line a public laughing stock under the noses of the ultra-conservative board.

Driver Larry Kemp climbed into the cab and exchanged a word or two with the departing Plymouth crew, who informed him that the Single was in peak condition and well enough for easier duties. George climbed into the cab and glanced at the fire and the dials –

all seemed to be well and little attention seemed necessary, apart from the normal maintenance of the fire. The guard's whistle, accompanied by his green flag, indicated that it was time to leave. They moved off gently. However, once they were away from Taunton, they discovered why the Singles - or at least their boilers - were being replaced; the engine was having to work quite hard on what was by modern standards only a moderate train weight. George found himself having to tend frequently to the fire to keep it hot enough for the locomotive to do its job, but on downhill runs he was pleased by both the speed and the smoothness that the pair of big driving wheels imparted. The cab did not jerk and sway to the degree expected on a regular locomotive with four or six coupled wheels, and he could see what it was that had so impressed the earlier engine crews. Aside from the need to keep the fire sufficiently well maintained for the driver to do his job, the run in the cab of this beautiful engine was for George both a pleasure and the fulfilment of a long-held ambition.

"These engines only handle light, fast trains," mused Driver Kemp.

"Why don't we have many such trains, Mr Kemp?" asked George.

"Passengers," replied his driver; "it's passengers that bring in the money. Remember, lad, that the GWR is a company like all private companies; it is there to make a profit for its shareholders as well as to provide a public service. It has to improve all the time and ensure that it operates efficiently. And a light train with 50 passengers needs the same size crew as a heavy express with 300 people on board. Which do you think is more profitable?"

"Mmmm, I see what you mean."

"Don't misunderstand me, George, I'm not suggesting any of that socialist nonsense that the government should run the railways. Our railways are generally run quite well; it's all done with large and small companies like ours, the LNWR, the Midland, the LSWR, the L&Y and so on. But if they don't make a profit, their shareholders lose the dividends. Not everyone lives near an omnibus route to travel, and these new-fangled motor cars you see on the roads these days are far too expensive for the likes of you and me."

"D'you think you'll ever drive a motor car, Mr Kemp?" asked George.

Larry Kemp laughed. "What, me? Drive a motor car? Why would I need one when we've got trains and buses, and where would I get the money to be able to buy one? No, mate, you need to be a toff with a big house in the country to buy - or even need - one of them. Most of the country gents have a pony and trap and find them quite sufficient for their purposes. This here," he added, patting the side of the cab, "is good enough for me!"

It was with considerable regret that they pulled into Swindon station, knowing that their lovely engine would go to the works and come out looking like neither fish nor fowl, and even then lasting only a few more brief years before it returned to go to the Swindon scrapyard.

Their disappointment was reduced rather when they found that their return shift was with an express to Penzance, crewing a Star class 4-6-0 heavy express locomotive. They were to take the train as far as Plymouth and George now knew that they would have a pilot engine to assist them over the South Devon banks. Their run was uneventful, apart from some amusement as they climbed

Wellington bank; here they crossed an up Paddington express, headed by a new Saint class 4-6-0, racing past them down the bank at high speed.

"If their engine's in good nick they're all trying to crack a hundred down here again," chuckled Larry, "ever since they reckon the *City of Truro* did it there, they all want to try. But they have to watch out that they don't get into Taunton too early or they'll run the risk of being carpeted for dangerous driving!"

"But how do they know what speed they're going?" asked George. "The engines don't have speedometers."

Larry smiled. "Most of us have a fair idea of what speed our train is doing; we count the mile posts as we pass them."

Waiting in Newton Abbot for their pilot engine, George smiled as he saw an oncoming passenger train pulling into the up platform. "Looks like they started to repaint the bufferbeam and were interrupted," he said, pointing to the blotched red bufferbeam on the locomotive.

"Where?" Larry came over to look, then his face paled. "That's not paint – it's dried blood! They've hit a cow, or even a person, and probably don't know it." He dropped off the cab and hurried over to the up locomotive; it was a 2-6-0 Mogul. He climbed into the cab and shortly afterwards the driver of the Mogul climbed down and went to examine the bufferbeam. He came back, nodding sadly to Larry.

"What now?" asked George as his driver returned to the cab.

Larry sighed. "They'll have to notify the police. The locomotive may be withdrawn for further examination and someone will have to go along down the line to see if they can find what they hit; a cow or a human body cannot stand being hit with a 300-tonne steel mallet at 50 miles an hour. The footplate crew will almost certainly be sent home. You can't drive safely if you know you've just killed somebody."

"But that's terrible!" George was aghast.

Larry shook his head. "Yes, it is, George, but it happens more often than you might think, and all enginemen have to be prepared for it to happen to them. The railways tend to keep quiet about it because it affects some men so badly they have to leave the footplate."

"But what can you do to prevent it happening?"

"That's the problem; nothing at all!"

"So you can kill someone without even seeing what you have done?"

"Yes, Fireman Denton, if you look at it that way. Welcome to railway service!"

5 - George is unimpressed with British Justice (April 1912)

Now that George Denton was a junior fireman, he was firing regularly on longer trips. He had been teamed with Driver Jem Hardcastle, who was a very shy but an amiable and elderly bachelor at Taunton shed. Jem was known to be relatively forgiving to his firemen and was always prepared to advise them. Under his tutelage, George learned the roads between Taunton, Chard, Minehead, Plymouth, Weston-super-Mare, and Bristol. He was beginning to thoroughly enjoy his new firing life when a spanner was suddenly and firmly thrown into the works.

They were sitting in the cab of a brand new small 45xx Prairie 2-6-2T at the head of the Minehead train, at the bay platform in Taunton, waiting for the connecting express from Bristol. Jem was smoking a cigarette and George was breaking up some of the larger lumps of coal in the bunker when two policemen walked up to their cab.

"Which of you is Driver Hardcastle?" the police sergeant called up.

Jem looked over from the cab. "That's me," he said, "why?"

"Come on down; you're needed at the nick to answer some questions."

"At the nick? What on earth for?" Jem was astounded.

"Where were you yesterday at about three o'clock in the afternoon?"

"I was having a cider or two with a couple of blokes in the local pub."

"And at half past three?"

"I was at home."

"Whose home?"

"Mine, of course."

"Your place close to Burleigh House, is it?"

"Burleigh House? Yes, it's about a mile away. Why?"

"Ever been in there?"

"No."

"You're sure about that?"

"Of course I'm sure."

"It would be on your way home from the pub."

"Yes."

"There was a burglary there yesterday and you were seen walking away from the place with a bag."

"I had a bag with my gear in it when I went home."

"What gear?"

"My lunchbox, an empty drink bottle, and a change of clothes. And I - what d'you mean 'walking away from the place'?"

"You were seen walking out of the drive to Burleigh House."

"That's nonsense; I walked right past it without stopping."

"Well, you'll have to explain all that to my inspector. Come with me."

The news went round the shed instantly. Fireman Jenkins, the shed gossip, raced around the shed with the news: "Hardcastle's been a-burglin' 'an 'ad 'is collar felt by the rozzers!" Many shook their heads in dismay; Jem Hardcastle was popular with his colleagues, who didn't want to believe what they were hearing. But two witnesses were adamant, and the stolen items had been found in Driver Hardcastle's house.

The trial concluded with a 'guilty' verdict. The defence lawyer was no match for the prosecutor, a well-known London silk, and Jem Hardcastle was given a prison sentence of three years. George was disappointed that so little character support had come from Jem's workmates; he decided that Taunton shed was not where he wanted to work, and he planned to start anew in a different environment, looking for another position elsewhere.

A firing job came up at Bristol's Bath Road shed, which George applied for and he was soon appointed there. He was teamed up with Driver Jock McKendrick, a man he took an instant dislike to and he soon discovered that the feeling was mutual. Driver McKendrick, not a Scot in spite of his name, was an unpleasant man; the almost permanent smile on his face hid a strong tendency to bully anyone unfortunate enough to be subordinate to him. This impacted especially on his firemen, who were required to follow the orders he gave in a peremptory manner. Driver McKendrick did not see himself as in any way responsible for assisting a fireman in the course of his duties. He was a very competent engine driver and demanded exacting standards from his firemen, but gave them no encouragement or advice at all. George looked forward greatly to any time he was not paired with McKendrick, but these occasions were regrettably few and far between.

Nevertheless, there were trips that George enjoyed in spite of his driver. One day, they found themselves on a Plymouth to Manchester train, which they had to take as far as Shrewsbury, via Hereford. As they waited on the platform at Temple Meads station, they were surprised to see the train headed by one of Mr Churchward's County class 4-4-0s. On his initial appointment Churchward had instituted a system of interchangeable parts with many of his engines, with the result that most cab crews found themselves at home in almost any cab, as these were often laid out in a very similar manner. Like George, McKendrick had not driven one of these engines but the cab layout, when they climbed in, was familiar. On leaving Bristol, McKendrick was careful as he eased the engine with its nine coaches on its way but he quickly got the feel of the locomotive and even, unusually for him, commented on the engine's performance.

"Seems like a good engine, this County, Fireman Denton; it's only a 4-4-0, not one of the new Star or Saint 4-6-0s, but it's obviously got plenty of power for its size."

George nodded at the comment, surprised that it was devoid of any snide remark or spiteful criticism of his firing.

"I wonder why we have a 4-4-0 on this train?" queried George, trying to take advantage of the unusually civil cab atmosphere.

"I heard it's because Shrewsbury to Hereford is a joint GW and LNWR route and LNWR doesn't want any heavy 4-6-0s on it."

"I see, Driver McKendrick, it's not too greedy on the coal, either."

"No, but just you make sure you keep the fire topped up - none of your usual slackness, mind."

The route through Hereford to Shrewsbury was a hilly one along the Welsh border, but the engine took the run in its stride, managing the gradients with rather more ease than the crew expected. In fact, the only adverse comment George could make about the new engine was that the ride was decidedly rough, not nearly as smooth as he was used to with 4-6-0s; more than once, his swing with coal on his shovel went wide, and the cab floor needed to be swept frequently.

"Can't you fire properly yet, Denton?" McKendrick's voice was heavy with sarcasm, and George got the distinct impression that his driver knew perfectly well why he was having difficulty; he was just enjoying the opportunity to pass a series of negative judgements. "Can't imagine how you managed to pass your firing exam." Followed a few minutes later by, "D'you want me to draw a big target round the firehole?"

This merciless tirade continued most of the way to Shrewsbury and George's patience was sorely tried as he attempted to keep the coal off the cab floor and into the appropriate areas of the fire.

"After that little display, Fireman Denton, I don't imagine you'll be taking your driving exam with any great success in the near future." Driver McKendrick was smiling as they climbed down from the cab of their County in Shrewsbury's Coleham shed. "You're lucky we weren't late in Salop, otherwise I'd have to write a report explaining that my fireman spent so much time cleaning the cab floor, he wasn't able to keep time!"

George was quietly seething; he knew that there was enough truth in what McKendrick said to convince the authorities that he wasn't ready for his driving exam. The fact of the matter, however, was that the County had been rougher in its riding than one would expect from a locomotive, and that their arrival on time had been largely due to his hard efforts with the shovel. The thought of more months – or even years - driving with McKendrick was almost too much to bear. Although admittedly a skilful driver, from whom much could be learned, George doubted whether he could keep his temper in the face of such consistent and unwarranted criticism.

For the next few months, George pondered the issue, wondering how he could both keep his cool and save his job. He was partly put at ease by comments made by other firemen who had fired to Driver McKendrick and who were equally unimpressed with his manner towards them. Yet George knew that sooner or later he would lose his cool, and that authority would be bound to support the senior driver's version in the event of any major disagreement, without supporting evidence to the contrary. He also knew that McKendrick was too smart to be caught out.

On their way from Bristol with a stopper one evening, George came to a decision; he had been told of a vacancy for a fireman at Wellington (Salop) and had initially rejected the idea of applying as he was happy in his digs and close to his parents. Wellington near Shrewsbury was a long way away, so he would need to find new digs and wouldn't be able to see his parents so often.

However, his decision was made when Driver McKendrick made a remark that George found particularly offensive. George had been in the tender, breaking up a large lump of coal, and a hole had developed in the fire before he could get back into the cab and fill it.

McKendrick had looked into the firebox. "Look at that great hole, Denton; you're bloody hopeless! We'll have to get rid of you like your old shed got rid of that bugger Hardcastle."

George, coal hammer in hand, glared at his driver; with a supreme effort, he put the hammer down, picked up his shovel, and filled the hole in the fire. He said nothing. Back in Bristol, he immediately wrote out an application for a transfer to Wellington. For the next three weeks, he ignored every remark of McKendrick's and only responded to a direct order.

To his great relief, in May his transfer came through. He was appointed to Wellington, where he found himself learning the roads to Crewe, Chester, Birmingham and Kidderminster. Although now further from his parents, he found life in the little Wellington shed far preferable to his time in Bristol.

One day in Shrewsbury, he saw the GWR crew taking over from the LNWR crew on a Manchester to Penzance express and was astonished to recognise his own father climbing into the cab. Henry told him he had been transferred to Bristol and would be on this train for several weeks. During September, George had a few minutes to exchange family gossip with his father on a daily basis, until the occasion when Henry Denton's fireman hurt himself too badly to continue. On arriving in Shrewsbury, he had been moving coal in the tender forward when a large lump fell on his arm and broke his wrist. Shrewsbury's Coleham shed did not have a spare fireman and George offered his services as he was off duty and was quite prepared to come back from Hereford on the cushions. The chance to fire to his father was too good to miss.

A phone call to Control that an emergency fireman was available as far as Hereford, and that the express would therefore not be delayed, ensured a rapid agreement from a relieved clerk, who did not realise the significance of the enginemen's names.

For George, firing to his father was a delight, but any ideas he had that his father would go easy on him were immediately abandoned. Henry Denton demanded care and skill from his fireman, but was full of good advice. Even his admonishments were issued with a twinkle in his eye, and father and son both immensely enjoyed the experience of working as a team. But the pleasure did not last; George was replaced as fireman at Ludlow. A locomotive inspector on the platform shook his head in disappointment. "I'm surprised at you, Henry," he said, "you know the Great Western doesn't allow members of the same family to work together in the cab."

"It was an emergency, Mr Naysmith," Henry replied, then, as the inspector strode off, he turned to George. "Sorry, son."

"But why, Dad? What's the problem with us both in the cab at the same time?"

"It's a strict rule; in the case of an accident, two males in a family could be wiped out." Then another thought occurred to him. "Oh, you didn't know; you remember Driver Hardcastle? He was freed from jail last week. They found that the witnesses had lied; one of them was apparently an ex-girlfriend of Jem's – seeking revenge for him dumping her. When her sister was appointed as assistant cook in Burleigh House, she used the opportunity. As she knew where Jem kept his spare key, putting the stuff in his house was easy."

"Well, what about the second witness?"

"Her sister, of course."

"But why didn't Mr Hardcastle's defence lawyer point all this out?"

"Apparently he tried to but the prosecutor was a top notch London QC and the defence lawyer was no match for him."

"So much for British justice," commented George grimly.

6 – An illusion shattered (October 1913)

It had been no secret that the late King Edward VII and his nephew Kaiser Wilhelm II had shown little love for each other, but the mutual dislike did not appear to have carried on to the same degree with the young George V. Nevertheless, there had been growing tension between the two monarchies: The Kaiser had declared that Germany too deserved its 'place in the sun', as it was described; the German Empire had been expanding rapidly over recent decades, and the Germans felt it needed the defence of a strong navy. This had been taken seriously amiss by British naval authorities, who believed themselves to be under threat, and over the previous ten years or so had been pouring vast sums into the development of a range of huge battleships which they called Dreadnoughts. The Germans had taken up the apparent challenge and were also building powerful warships. However, in spite of the increasing tensions in national diplomacy, generally relations between the British and German navies, among the officers and men, were cordial. There were commonly exchange visits, and in the Far East the two navies, with the French, Russians and Japanese, often made common cause, particularly against the Chinese, who had the infernal cheek to want to remove the 'foreign devils' and control affairs in their own country.

Within the Great Western Railway, Driver Leonard Baxendale of Wellington shed was far more interested in his new fireman than foreign affairs. He had watched as George Denton climbed into the cab and introduced himself before checking the gauges and the condition of the fire, slipping a couple of shovelfuls of coal exactly where they were needed; he had already used the watering hose to wet the coal, all to the good.

"Right ho, George, let's get started," Driver Baxendale said.

"Ready when you are, Mr Baxendale," came the reply.

"No, George, not Mr Baxendale. I'm Len to you; we don't stand on ceremony in my cab."

George nodded: "Len!" He was pleased. He'd had had a variety of drivers since the unpleasant Jock McKendrick, but Len seemed like an easy-going man. It remained to be seen what he was like as a driver.

Their first job was to be an unfitted freight of empty coal wagons to Gresford colliery and continuing from there with a full coal train to Birkenhead. Their engine was one of the 2-6-0 Moguls, with outside frames and inside cylinders, which gave them a somewhat old-fashioned appearance. They were known as Aberdares, so called because they were originally designed for the South Wales coal traffic.

Len's and George's coal train was now slowing down on the approach to Wrexham. As they neared the starter signal at the end of the platform at Wrexham they saw a naval officer standing on the platform, waving to them.

"I bet he wants a lift to Birkenhead," said Len to his fireman, "tell him to hop on, George, but we can't stop."

George signalled to the officer to jump on as they passed at walking speed. "Thanks lads, I missed the train I was supposed to catch and need to get to my destroyer; we're steaming to Pompey this evening."

"Pompey?" queried George in surprise, thinking of his Latin lessons at school, as the starter dropped and Len increased speed; the wagons began to rattle as the couplings started to snatch gently and he had to speak up. "Why would you want to get to Italy?"

"Ah, no, Pompey's what we naval types call Portsmouth. Er - you won't get into trouble, taking me in your cab, will you?"

"Not if Control doesn't know about you," said Len with a grin. "George here won't tell on you, will you George?"

"Not me, Len!"

"There you go, you're quite safe. But we'll have to drop you off where officialdom won't spot you. We're not supposed to carry passengers. I'll slow down at Rockferry and you'll have to take an electric train on to Birkenhead."

"Yes, I realise that, thanks very much. After Pompey, my ship's off on a friendly visit to the French navy at La Rochelle, and then I'm to train at the Naval Gunnery School. The navy is worried about the Germans using their big airships, the Zeppelins, to drop bombs on us if there's a war."

"Been in the navy long, then?" asked Len.

"I joined at Dartmouth as a twelve-year-old, fifteen years back. My dad's a copper and didn't want me in the police force. He was once part of the Royal bodyguard in the old King's time," the officer added proudly.

"The First Gentleman of Europe?" queried George, impressed. King Edward VII had been referred to as such in respect of his status as Emperor of the world's largest empire.

The officer chuckled. "My dad would laugh to hear you say that! He used to call him the 'First Lecher of Europe', he had so many women. All very quiet, of course; the newspapers weren't allowed to mention any of his affairs."

George was shocked. "Affairs? You mean the King had – er - relationships with other women?"

The officer shrugged his shoulders. "I'm sorry to disillusion you."

"But-?"

"It all apparently started when he was a young officer cadet at Sandhurst," said the officer, "his mates organised a young lady of what you might call doubtful virtue for him at a party, and he never looked back."

"But what about after he was married to Queen Alexandra?"

"Oh dear, fella, you *do* have a lot to learn!"

George shook his head in disbelief; that fine, dignified man having affairs with loose women! This wasn't what he had learned at school at all.

The engine slowed before Rockferry as they came up to a home signal at danger; it clanged down to the 'clear' position but before Len lifted the regulator he nodded at the officer and said, "Now would be a good time to hop off. The station's only a couple of hundred yards away."

"Many thanks indeed, lads, I'm much obliged to you both!" He slipped off the cab steps and walked across the field, heading for the nearby road.

George glanced across the cab at Len. "Do footplatemen often give illegal cab lifts to non-railwaymen?"

"Well, of course it's not permitted, but I tend to make an exception for the services. I think they deserve a bit of consideration. I was in the navy briefly during the Boer War and I know what conditions onboard ship can be like." George was not to know that 31 years later he would give a lift to an American airman under rather grimmer circumstances.

As they rumbled through Rockferry on the down slow, they were passed by a short express parcels from Birkenhead, accelerating out of the station; it was hauled by a Dean Single wheeler.

"Look at that!" said George, smiling, "marvellous-looking engines, those!"

Len nodded, "I'll give you that, but you wouldn't want to fire one with anything heavy on its tail. Fifteen years ago they could handle most duties, but these days trains are much heavier and the Singles don't cope too well."

"That's true enough," agreed George, "I fired one three years back and it was hard work except for the downhill running."

There was a sudden *crack!* and the gauge glass split, spouting steam and boiling water into the cab. Instantly, George and Len leaped out of the cab, hanging on to the handrails for grim death until the water flow ceased. They still had enough to reach Birkenhead, where George could change the gauge glass in peace.

"Right, lad," said Len, "let's leave them to it, get into the enginemen's mess, and get some grub inside us. Then we'll find our engine for the return run."

They were enjoying a cup of tea and their sandwiches when one of the shed lads poked his head in the door; "Are you the Wellington crew off the Gresford coal?"

"That's us," Len looked at the youngster, "what's up, lad?"

"We've got a big engine and Stafford Road wants it back smartish. Ye're to take it back light engine. It's ready but yer'll just 'ave to turn it on the table before yer take it back."

Len's eyes gleamed. "That'll be that Saint the Stafford Road boss was cursing about yesterday. Judging from its number, it's almost brand new and he doesn't want to lose sight of it. I bet he's been on the phone raising Cain and demanding its quick return before Chester or Salop get their hands on it."

"We're taking a Saint light engine back to Wolverhampton?" George's face lit up. Running with an express locomotive without a train was unusual; the GWR accountants didn't like the idea of using a lot of coal just to run 120 tonnes of engine and tender without making any profit from the business. But for the engine crew, running a big new express engine without any coaches on its tail was almost certain to be an unalloyed pleasure. Once it was up to speed, the fireman could relax in a manner that would allow him to even sit down and enjoy the view for long minutes at a time.

They reached the engine and it was indeed the Saint 4-6-0 that Len had expected. Len climbed the cab steps before his fireman. "George, have you ever driven a big engine for a previous driver?"

"Once or twice; why?"

"I'll give you the regulator somewhere along the run back. Now go and get your tootsie on the edge of the table and yell when she's balanced."

George climbed down and walked to the edge of the turntable, waited until Len had gently moved the locomotive onto it, then put his foot on the edge. The table rail end was a couple of inches lower than the ground rail end and it gradually rose as Len eased the engine towards the middle. "Right!" called George as the two rail ends were at the same level; this showed that the engine was nicely balanced, making it much easier for them to push the table round with one man at each end.

They were not disappointed at the return run; the huge engine, with its six-foot-eight-and-a-half-inch driving wheels ran effortlessly. Indeed, the only problem they had was to ensure that they held the speed down, in order not to catch up with the preceding Paddington parcels; this would have had them braking or stopping at signals along the route and giving them an uneven ride.

They slowed down as they ran round the Chester, avoiding tracks from the Birkenhead line to the LNWR North Wales lines, and headed to Saltney Junction where they joined the main GWR line to the south. George was given the regulator between Ruabon and Baschurch and their run into Wolverhampton's Stafford Road shed was with the thrill of controlling a speeding monster. Their return on the cushions to Wellington was something of an anti-climax after their run from Birkenhead.

George never forgot that first run with a light engine in top notch condition. It confirmed for him that he had, like his father, made the right choice of career.

7 – 'To err is human' (April 1914)

The Great Western Railway was on something of a roll. Its engines were among the finest and most efficient in the country (although Mr Bowen-Cooke's big LNWR Claughtons were beginning to make a name for themselves, and a Mr Ivatt of the Great Northern had produced a 4-4-2 Atlantic, which was gaining a fine reputation), the safety record of the company was second to none, and recent route shortenings from Paddington had increased rivalry between the company and the competing London and North Western to Birmingham, as well as the London and South Western to the West Country.

The GWR had largely recovered from its financial burden of closing its broad gauge system in 1892 and was now paying a regular and pleasing dividend to its shareholders. Altogether, it was a company that most of its employees were proud to work for.

Things were not quite so rosy in the Paddington headquarters, however; senior officials there, as in most of the major railway companies, were concerned with how they would manage their systems in the case of a European war, which was looking increasingly likely. A government takeover of major railway managements was mooted, and all the railway companies were warned to prepare for such a possibility.

However, such worries had not filtered down to the footplatemen of the various companies. Driver Len Baxendale nodded to himself in satisfaction; his first impression of his new fireman had, in his opinion, been confirmed. The man really knew what he was about; he was quietly efficient in his managing of the steam pressure, while at the same time looking after the many other duties required. He was short but stocky and had no difficulty in swinging his loaded coal shovel around for a couple of hours at a time without much in the way of a break. But what surprised Len most was the fact that the cab was usually spotless when George was in action; how he managed to stay relatively clean was a mystery to Len, who wasn't averse to a bit of dirt in his work. Life in a steam locomotive cab was not conducive to keeping a man clean: firstly, the coal dust tended to get everywhere and had to be constantly hosed down with the coal watering pipe and then there was the oiling that had to be done before a locomotive could be taken out of the shed; the oil had to be frequently topped up en route as well. The combination of steam, smoke, oil, coal, ash and sweat did not give rise to clean work clothes. How George managed to keep himself almost as clean coming off shift as he had been going on puzzled Len no end. Yet there was no doubt that George was unusually fastidious about his appearance: his tie was correctly tied, his shirt was clean, as were his overalls; his shoes were polished daily, and in spite of his vigorous work with the coal shovel, his hands were normally clean.

After months working with Fireman Denton, Len was very much at ease with him (and was even finding himself checking his own clothing and shoes before coming on duty). He found he could relax and take a turn on the shovel, happily leaving the driving to his fireman on runs where there were no tricky sections which required an experienced driver. A word or two here and there sufficed for

George to quickly pick up Len's driving tips; it was if he only needed guidance on matters which were new to him. Perhaps he had inherited some of his dad's skill by a kind of osmosis, thought Len sometimes, such was the speed that George acquired new abilities.

But there was more to it than just this, mused Len; he had noticed once or twice that George appeared to be almost psychic. Once when George was driving, they were approaching a small station on a curve and George lowered the regulator to gradually bring the train to a halt, but before Len could comment that they were slowing down earlier than was necessary, they rounded the curve and saw on the platform that a luggage trolley had been left without its brake on; it was rolling towards the platform edge, from where it tumbled onto their track. George was able to stop the train just in time to avoid hitting the fallen trolley. Len stared in amazement at George. "How the holy hell did you know that was going to happen?"

George shrugged; "I couldn't see the platform and wasn't sure how far away it was."

"Yes but-?" Len shook his head and continued, "Well, all I can say is that you were bloody lucky; or rather *we* were bloody lucky!"

However, George and Len's luck - if that's what it was - ran out a few weeks later. They were taking a short fitted goods towards Hereford and were accelerating out of Craven Arms when they felt a shock under the wheels of their locomotive, a Bulldog class 4-4-0. At first they didn't understand exactly what had happened but Len instantly dropped the regulator and applied the engine brakes; the train began to slow and then they heard a clattering from the rear. "We're off the road!" shouted Len as the train stopped. They looked back to see several of the vans derailed, three leaning dangerously close to their track.

"Quick, George, run ahead and wave down any oncoming train! It might hit those vans!"

George jumped down onto the track and began to race ahead to the next signal box to warn the bobby there, but he was too late. A stopping passenger was approaching him, so he stopped and waved frantically at the driver of the tank engine. The train immediately began to slow as its driver applied the brakes, but he was too late to avoid an accident and the engine hit the derailed vans. The engine came off the track but luckily stayed upright; the first coach derailed and tipped over on its side. The three following coaches also derailed but stayed more or less vertical, leaving the remaining four coaches undamaged. The guard of the passenger train jumped out and ordered George to run to the next signal box to report the accident so that the bobby could protect his section. George ran ahead once more and reached the box, which was another half-mile on; he reported the accident and the signalman phoned his colleagues both up and down the line, to stop any other traffic in both directions. In the meantime, George returned to the scene of the accident, where the Craven Arms police and ambulances were also in action, helping the fourteen injured. Three dead passengers had already been covered and gently laid to one side.

Clearing the wreckage with the breakdown gang from Salop took a day and a half; inspection showed that the cause of the derailment was a misaligned rail end. The fishplate joining two abutting rails had been removed by a permanent way repair gang, in order that a damaged rail could be replaced. After the new rail had been laid, the end chairs had not been bolted back in position, leaving the rail only loosely connected to its neighbour. Len and George's train, the first one over the repaired section, had pushed the unsecured rail out of alignment and derailed. The fault lay squarely on the shoulders of the permanent way gang and especially on its foreman, whose job it was to check the work done by his men. A basic rule of safety had been ignored and as a consequence three people had died and fourteen were in hospital, none of them railway employees.

Len and George were deeply shocked by the episode but were still required to report back at work the next day to give a detailed report of the accident. Neither of the two locomotives was badly damaged. They had been re-railed by the breakdown crane gang and were towed back to Shrewsbury shed.

Both crewmen were scheduled by the shed foreman on lighter duties for the following two weeks; they were put on stopping passenger trains to Crewe via Market Drayton and Nantwich. This short Great Western branch actually ended at Nantwich but trains generally went through the little market town another couple of miles to Crewe, where the GWR maintained a small shed at Gresty Lane, in fact a sub-shed to Wellington.

Arriving for the first time at the huge Crewe station, George and Len found themselves surrounded in the bay by LNWR engines and admired their smart, shiny black paint and plum-and-white coaches, reminiscent of the Great Western's previous colour scheme of brown and cream, now being replaced by all over red-brown. George felt that this was a retrograde step as he thought the brown and cream with the green of the engines looked magnificent. But then, he mused, he was only a lowly fireman and had no say in the matter. His views were, however, echoed by many members of the public who had become used to the GWR tradition.

Crewe, with its huge locomotive works, was the focal point of the LNWR and the junction of six main routes to London, Scotland, Liverpool, Manchester, North Wales and Hereford. The LNWR called itself the Premier Line; it was Britain's biggest railway and widely believed to be the world's largest private company.

As they pulled into Crewe from Wellington with their local stopping train, George smiled to himself, thinking that with their little Stella class 2-4-0 locomotive standing next to one of the handsome LNWR Prince of Wales class 4-4-0s, the GWR was trying to thumb its nose at the LNWR, implying that Crewe didn't deserve any of the Great Western's more modern engines. Wellington shed rarely had anything bigger. Nevertheless, as he watched, a brand new Claughton class 4-6-0 pulled in with the down Scottish Express. Len leaned over and pointed it out. "Now that, George my lad, is the North Western's answer to our Stars. They're said to be well able to handle the heaviest expresses. Perhaps they learned something from the exchange four years back, allowing our Star into Euston, when we showed them what a real locomotive could do! They loaned us one of their Experiment class 4-6-0s but it didn't impress."

George nodded. "I heard that and wondered why; even the North Western enginemen don't think much of the Experiments. One of the North Western men in Chester said they were unreliable; when you get into one, you don't know whether it will pull well or let you down. Apparently, they're also hard to fire."

Curiously, as they spoke, a southbound express crawled into the station, drawn by one of the Experiments. Judging from its efforts, the engine was in serious trouble as it came slowly to a stand. The fireman climbed down and began to uncouple the coaches. Once this was completed, the engine drew forward; it was apparently being withdrawn for examination.

"There you go, George," said Len, "if our humble platelayers can make a mistake, so can the top engine designers of the LNWR!"

This remark was overheard by a gentleman on the platform who was standing and shaking his head at their little engine. "You're quite wrong about that, lads," he said, "we sent the Experiment to your lot knowing full well it wouldn't perform." He was a benign-looking gentleman, with a bushy moustache and a smile that set the two of them at ease.

"But why?" Len asked him. "That doesn't make sense!"

"Oh but it does," replied the man. "For a while, we weren't permitted to build good, high-performing engines which cost the company money, so when the Experiment shamed the LNWR, the board relented and allowed us to build something better."

As they were talking, another new Claughton passed them, heading south; it stopped and then backed across the tracks on to the coaches of the London-bound express and gently buffered up to them. The fireman coupled the locomotive up and when the whistle blew, it moved off effortlessly with its heavy train.

The man nodded in the direction of the fast disappearing train. "Now that," he said with satisfaction, "is an engine which would give your Stars a run for their money!"

George and Len were, in spite of themselves, deeply impressed. Len leaned out of the cab. "Er, who are you?" he asked curiously.

"Me?" said the man vaguely. "Oh, I'm employed at the Works here." He strode off before they could ask any more questions.

"Wonder who he is?" said George.

"D'you know," said Len thoughtfully, "I think we've been talking to Mr Bowen-Cooke. He's the Chief Mechanical Engineer of the LNWR!"

8 – A capital sight (September 1915)

The year had been disappointing; the war had not gone the way many of the prophets had predicted: the German Empire had not been beaten by the previous Christmas, indeed it had shown itself to be rather more successful than the Entente Cordiale, although its advance had, to some extent, been stemmed, and Paris had not fallen. Horror stories of the experiences of troops in the trenches had begun to filter through, in spite of the attempts of the military authorities to hide the truth of the dreadful losses that both sides were experiencing.

The government was constantly demanding more men to fill the gaps fast appearing in the armies in northern France and Belgium, and many railwaymen were signing on. So far, George had only made one attempt to try to enlist; but as a member in a reserved occupation, he could not be called up; he could only join the army if he had permission from his boss, who had point-blank refused. "Out of the question Fireman Denton; we've already lost far too many enginemen. Your duty is here to support the war effort by running the troop and ammunition trains which the country so urgently needs!"

George had been happy working with Len Baxendale for the previous couple of years and felt that he had learned a great deal from his driver's expertise, but his pangs of guilt that he wasn't fighting for his country were rapidly overcoming any feeling that firing steam locomotives was helping his country's war effort. There was a vacancy for a fireman at Chester and George applied for it, with a view to working there for a month or two before requesting permission to join the army, in the hope that a different shed foreman might allow him to sign up. His application was accepted and he moved to digs in the northern city. Here he had to learn the roads to Birkenhead, West Kirby, Dolgellau, Blaenau Ffestiniog, and Manchester Exchange, all destinations to which the GWR ran its trains, some of them in connection with the LNWR.

It was during his brief time in Chester that he found himself on a Paddington train. He and elderly Driver Monty Beacham were due to return from Shrewsbury on a stopper when their duty was altered; they were told that due to a staffing shortage they were to take a London train and stay overnight in a railwaymen's hostel and return the following day. Fortunately, Monty knew the road quite well and was able to warn George about where important signals were situated. The run was uneventful and they arrived in Paddington in the late afternoon. After an extra long shift, Monty went straight to the hostel, but they were allowed to sleep in the following day and could take an early afternoon train back to Chester, so George used this opportunity of his first visit to the capital to pay a call on friends of his parents who had moved to North London some years previously.

He also wanted to have a look at the electric locomotives of the Metropolitan Railway which were now running to Uxbridge via Harrow, where his parents' friends lived. George was already familiar with electric traction from his visits to the Mersey Railway, with its American-style cars, but these had electric motors under some of the cars and were controlled by the driver from the front. The Liverpool Overhead Railway, supplying a valuable service to the Liverpool dockyard workers, had similar arrangements. George had heard that the Metropolitan Railway had traditional coaches which could be hauled by either electric or steam locomotives, and he was keen to see how this system worked.

He caught his train at Baker Street, after admiring the chunky lines of the big, dark red-and-brown electric locomotive, and boarded one of the teak coaches of the train. As he sat, he wondered briefly what it would be like to drive an electric locomotive, secure in the knowledge that his collar would be clean right through his shift; and whether sitting down on the job would actually satisfy him. He concluded that it wouldn't. George was by nature an active man and the thought of spending the whole day on a seat did not appeal in the least. Nevertheless, the acceleration of the train on starting was astounding and George realised that a steamer - even in prime condition and with an efficient crew - could hardly match that of this electric locomotive. Furthermore, the general cleanliness of the surroundings was something else steam could not be expected to provide.

George spent a pleasant evening reminiscing with his parents' friends and was waiting at the station for his train back to London, forgetting for a time all about the war. His mind was brought back to it, however, in a sudden, dramatic manner; he heard a curious rumbling sound from somewhere above him. With other passengers, he glanced upwards to see searchlights probing the clouds; there was a distant *rat-tat-tat* sound, and aircraft could be seen high up.

George wondered what on earth they were firing at until he glimpsed a huge, grey cigar-shaped form above the planes, gliding through the night clouds. It was outlined by the searchlights but was clearly higher than the fighters. They couldn't quite reach it, and their firing was consequently ineffective.

The waiting passengers had heard dull thumps further north and assumed they were thunder, but now realised it was the sound of the Zeppelin dropping its bombs. It was now returning after its bombing raid, unscathed by the frantic efforts of the Royal Flying Corps aircraft. However, the groans from the crowd turned to cries of delight; one of the fighters had somehow managed to get close beneath the Zeppelin and fired a flare up at it. The flare had reached the rear of the airship and the gas bag caught fire. The fire spread quickly along the envelope of the airship; one end of the gondola dangled wildly as one of its supporting struts broke and three crewmen were thrown out. The figures fell downwards, to gasps from the watching spectators; they plunged straight to earth with no chance of survival. An engine strut also snapped and the engine plummeted, its propeller spinning madly, into a nearby field where it exploded. The Zeppelin was by now an inferno and sank slowly to the ground about a mile or so distant. A couple of lorries could be seen hurrying to the site as well as an ambulance, but George seriously doubted that anyone could be saved from the burning wreckage. He had at that moment no feeling of glee at the destruction of the airship, or the deaths of the crew; he was horrified at the thought of the crewmen being burned alive or falling helplessly to their deaths, although several of the nearby observers on the station didn't seem to share his views. There were raucous cheers at the downfall of one of what the newspapers were calling the Babykillers, due to the somewhat indiscriminate bombing the Zeppelins were responsible for.

While George strongly approved of the attack on the airship, he was deeply disturbed by the dreadful deaths which the crewmen had suffered. He had never given much thought to the consequences to the individuals involved in the actual fighting; now this was brought home to him with a vengeance. He began to see the war in a rather different light, wondering what it would be like to be thrown out of an aircraft thousands of feet in the air. He knew that parachutes were used by observers in balloons spotting for artillery; whenever enemy aircraft were seen approaching, the observers would jump out of their baskets and parachute down to safety, their ground crew trying to winch the balloon down before the aircraft could shoot it. George had also heard that parachutes were not given to aircraft pilots because they might be tempted to jump out even in the case of minor damage. He travelled back to his London hostel in a troubled frame of mind.

Back in Chester the following evening, George noted from the shift board that he and his driver were booked to take a Manchester to Penzance express from Salop to Bristol. He hoped he would get a chance to catch up with his father once more and hear some family gossip. Their engine was one of Mr Churchward's Bulldog class 4-4-0s, which were regarded as being quite strong enough for the duty; but this one was due for an overhaul which, on account of the war, had not yet been carried out. As a result, it rode roughly; this was disappointing because these engines had a reputation for smooth riding. As they pulled away from the station and headed south past the huge signalbox on to the Hereford line, it was already clear that this engine was going to be tricky to fire. Driver Jack Murgatroyd was unable to keep his position on the little shelf which passed for a driver's seat in all Great Western engines; he had to stand holding on to the regulator and swearing. George too had difficulty in throwing the coal accurately into the firebox, and many a shovelful ended on the cab floor when the shovel hit the side of the firehole as the engine jerked. He was kept busy at the station stops, clearing up the scattered coal, and Driver Murgatroyd took over the firing two or three times to give George a breather on the regulator for a few miles.

Arriving at Temple Meads station, they uncoupled the locomotive and took it to Bath Road shed for servicing. While his driver checked their return schedule, George scouted round the shed to see if he might catch up with his father. Both men were to be disappointed: George discovered Harry Denton was away on a Newton Abbot turn, and Jack Murgatroyd came back with a gloomy face.

"We're taking our Bulldog back to Salop in an hour's time," he said, "we have a Plymouth to Liverpool empty troop train back as far as Salop, where North Western men will take over. We go back to Chester on the cushions."

"Well, Jack," said George sardonically, "that should get me fit."

"It'll also get you knackered," said his driver, "but I'll give you a hand again, of course."

Their return trip was almost a mirror image of their outward run; the engine was still just as rough and although the train was made up of empty coaching stock, the eleven coaches made it a heavy train for the 4-4-0. Both men were exceedingly tired on arrival at Chester Shed. The foreman the next day was sympathetic but with crew shortages, he had to put them on another long run with an overnight stay at a hostel; they were to take a mid-day Birkenhead express to Paddington.

"Look on the bright side, Fireman Denton," he said to George, "you don't have to be back here until tomorrow evening, so you can sleep in, and before you take the 2.10pm back you'll have time to have another look at some of the sights in the capital."

"Thank you for the suggestion, sir," replied George, "but I've seen one capital sight already and that was enough for me."

9 - Private Denton (August 1916)

Fireman George Denton had for some time been increasingly concerned at the war situation and he felt troubled that he was not taking a more active part in it. It had not been a good couple of months in France; the British army was not only bogged down, it had suffered a major setback following what had clearly been undue optimism on the part of senior leadership in both Paris and Westminster. The newspapers made depressing reading for those who had confidently anticipated an Allied breakthrough of the German lines in northern France. The Battle of the Somme was not going well and British casualties were mounting rapidly, with no sign of success.

Criticism of the government was increasing; the population wanted to know why the Germans were not being defeated by the immense efforts on the part of Allied Command. Although the Americans were making sympathetic noises, no serious military assistance was forthcoming. All in all, there did not appear to be room for much optimism. Indeed, the only recent success was the much trumpeted defeat of a German fleet off Jutland in the North Sea, yet even that was being questioned.

It seemed that the German Navy had inflicted much heavier damage on British battleships and battle-cruisers than they had themselves received. There were rumours of an inherent weakness in the design of the gun turret shafts in British capital ships, some of which had exploded after what had seemed to be lucky hits. There was, admittedly, news of what appeared to be a minor success in the Middle East, where an Arab revolt against the Turks was taking place, and a junior British officer called Lawrence was mentioned, but since few had ever heard of the Hejaz or knew where it was, little was made of it.

Waiting for the guard's green flag at Baschurch on a semi-fast to Chester, George noticed a confrontation between an elegantly dressed young lady in her early 20s and a dapper young man sitting on a platform seat. The girl put her hand into her purse and took out a white feather then handed it without a word to the young man. Several other people nearby noted her action and nodded in approval. The young man, however, took the feather with a smile and, thanking the young woman, stuck it into the band of his hat. He then turned and picked up the walking stick which was hooked over the back of the seat behind him and, using the stick to help him stand, lifted his hat politely to the girl. He raised his trouser turn-up slightly to show a wooden leg, which he tapped with his walking stick. "Little disagreement with a German soldier at Cambrai last year," he said before limping away.

A soldier standing nearby addressed the young lady: "I was wounded on the Somme five weeks back and I was ferried back to the First Aid station in an ambulance driven by a young woman; she would have been about your age, Miss. Seems to me you'd better keep those white feathers for those like yourself."

The girl's face turned bright red and she hurried away.

The whole incident made a deep impression on George and for the rest of his shift he was deep in thought. As a railway fireman, he was in a reserved occupation and could not be conscripted into the army without the permission of his boss, who had already twice refused to consider such a request from him. George decided to try again, but this time he proposed to use a subterfuge. The Chester shedmaster was a very practical man, who much preferred to have a tool or a locomotive regulator in his hands; he was impatient with the necessary clerical work his job required of him. All the footplatemen knew this and were usually reluctant to involve themselves in any incident which required a written report. George therefore waited for his opportunity until a foggy day produced three incidents; all minor but which nevertheless needed to be reported; he made an offer to the affected drivers to write out their reports, have the drivers sign them, and he, George, would take them to the foreman for his signature. The enginemen were duly grateful and the three reports were neatly handwritten and signed by the relevant enginemen. George waited outside the foreman's office until he could see that the man was busy with his paperwork and then he knocked and entered the office.

"Sorry, sir," he said, "a few more short reports for you to sign."

"What are they?" demanded the foreman.

"All very minor, sir, but they still need your signature."

"Let's have them, then." The foreman signed the four papers that George passed to him, giving only the first two a cursory glance before turning back to a lengthy report. "Put those in my out-tray, Fireman Denton, thank you." George nodded, placing three of the papers in the tray. He slid the last paper unobtrusively into his pocket and left.

This fourth paper was a signed application for George to leave the

GWR and join the army.

George's introduction to the army was not an experience he enjoyed. Their elderly sergeant, who had clearly seen plenty of active service, was a hard case. George had expected this, yet Sergeant McPherson, wounded in France, had a special talent for making his charges' lives a misery. During the three weeks of solid drill, the 30 young recruits tried hard to obey instantly his every command, but McPherson still found minute imperfections in whatever they did. No matter that they had cleaned their uniforms, polished their boots till they were gleaming, dressed their ranks as straight as a ruler, their sergeant pointed out some fault every time. At the moment he was standing at the edge of the parade ground, under the shade of some horse chestnut trees, while his trainees were at attention in the centre.

"Wot the 'ell's 'e doin'?" muttered the lad next to George out of the corner of his mouth.

"Can't see," whispered George in an equally careful reply; the sergeant seemed to be picking something off the ground.

"It'll be summat to annoy us wiv at any rate."

Sergeant McPherson marched over once more and walked along the front rank, inspecting them. He stopped in front of George.

"You've dropped a bollock, 'aven't you, soldier?" he said grimly.

"Don't think so, sergeant," replied George cautiously. He had taken extra care with his uniform and boots that morning.

"Yes you 'ave, Private Denton," McPherson said and he held up a pale cream, peeled conker for all to see, "'cause I've found it!"

The whole squad hooted with laughter, but the sergeant roared, "Right, you lot! Laughing on parade! Three days' CB!"

The recruits stopped laughing, shocked.

Three days Confined to Barracks was not funny.

The training sessions became progressively shorter as the front lines in France swallowed increasing numbers of troops. The lads' final day came several weeks later and while they were waiting for the transport to take them out of the camp, Sergeant McPherson came over to George.

"Private Denton, I gave you a particularly hard time," he said.

"Your job, I believe, Sergeant," said George in surprise.

"Yes, and you took it well. Tell me, are you a god-fearing man?"

"Er- not really, Sergeant, why?"

"You may not believe in heaven, lad; but when you get to the front in Belgium or France, you'll find that hell exists. Look after yourself, young Denton."

After three months in the front line, George understood only too clearly what Sergeant McPherson had meant. Hell certainly existed and he, Private George Denton, was right in the middle of it. He had been over the top with fixed bayonet countless times and had already seen three of his officers killed. He had learned that forming friendships with other soldiers was not worthwhile as battlefield life expectancy was too short. He himself had shot or bayoneted several enemy soldiers and had discovered that a thrust with his entrenching shovel under enemy chins if he had dropped his rifle was an effective emergency defence. Invariably, he felt sick after taking part in the mindless brutality of an attack. He dreaded the whistle but went out every time, wondering whether he would get back in one piece.

On one attack, they had cleared the German trench and were retreating when he slipped in the mud, just as common in the German trenches as their own, and fell awkwardly, hitting his head on a beam and knocking himself out cold. When he regained consciousness, he was still dizzy and disoriented. All was quiet and he was being carried on a stretcher. *I must have been picked up and brought back to...* he thought, then he stared; the soldiers carrying him were wearing grey uniforms with *Pickelhaube* helmets. They took him into a bunker displaying a Red Cross flag, and an army doctor came over and spoke to the soldiers, presumably telling them where to put George. They placed him in a clean bed and went out. There were nine other soldiers in neighbouring beds, one of whom was another Tommy.

The doctor came to George's bed and stared into his eyes, pulling back the lids. He nodded to himself and then addressed George. "You haff luck," he said in heavily accented English, "your wound iss not bad, chust - *wie heisst das bloss-?*" he sought the English word, "- concussion. We keep you today; check your head. Tomorrow you go to prison camp." He went on to examine his other patients. Shortly afterwards, all were brought food: black bread, sausage and what George thought might have been a form of coffee. He found the taste of the food strange but it was nevertheless welcome. One of the wounded German soldiers handed round some cigarettes and although George didn't smoke, he took one anyway, nodding his thanks, as did the other wounded Tommy, who lit up gratefully.

The doctor's words were prophetic: George was lucky. The

following dawn there was another British attack before he could be transferred to the prisoner-of-war camp, and in the confusion George was able to join the attacking soldiers in their withdrawal. He was back with his own unit within 24 hours. Discussing his capture with a young officer, he commented on his surprise that he was treated just like wounded German soldiers.

"Yes," nodded the officer, "that's what most of our blokes say if we get them back."

"I had heard they were brutal," said George.

"You've been reading our propaganda material," replied the officer angrily, "d'you know, when the war began, we were told German soldiers ate Belgian children for breakfast! If I had my way, I'd have the people who wrote that rubbish shot, and I'd ban any politician from having any say in voting for war unless he was prepared to put himself or his son in the front line. That'd make the buggers think!" He paused; "Mind you, I've heard that German propaganda can be full of lies too. Er-sorry! Look, Private Denton; you didn't hear me say all that."

"No Sir," replied George. He'd already made his own mind up about what the German soldiers were like; he'd seen them in their own trenches and apart from their uniforms and food, they weren't any different from him and his mates.

Back in Chester shed the shedmaster was still fuming at the loss of such a promising engineman; he might be in control of the work of almost 200 men but even he couldn't reject a formal army demand. He was, however, far more diligent in perusing carefully every form presented to him for signing.

10 - A dangerous assignment (May 1917)

Private Denton was with the rest of his platoon, being rested some miles from the front after being on the receiving end of two months in the trenches. His company had suffered more than 50 per cent losses from enemy shelling and attacks but had neither retreated nor advanced from their positions. This seemed to be the norm for most of the front line on both sides of their sector. The war had apparently reached some kind of bloody stalemate, with no gains for the continuing immense cost in men's lives on both sides.

What remained of their platoon was waiting in Boulogne harbour as reinforcements arrived from the UK. They were relaxing as far as was possible, given the distant sounds of shelling that could occasionally be heard. Lance Corporal Harrison was waiting with three other soldiers to lead the new men to where they could be given their instructions. But after they were seen by Lieutenant Bridewell, Harrison wanted to impress on them some of the unofficial guidelines for life in the trenches; he was hoping some of them would survive the next six weeks. George and two other men had been volunteered by Harrison to back up his advice. L/Cpl Harrison had been fighting for over two years, which in itself was something of a miracle, so his advice was considered to be worth listening to. Lt Bridewell's instructions to the recruits standing smartly at attention had concerned the need for showing proper respect to officers and NCOs, and for washing their socks regularly. After the Lieutenant left, Harrison stood the new lads at ease and his advice concentrated on the need for staying alive, which required careful maintenance of their rifles and bayonets, keeping their heads out of sight of enemy snipers, and looking after any mates injured in the attacks. He left the squad and, before they could move away, George stood up and said quietly, "Listen lads, what the officer says is important, of course, but what L/Cpl Harrison says'll help you survive here for more than three weeks."

As the train backed into the siding where the men were waiting, George stared at the locomotive; it didn't look like the French engines he had seen before and there was something familiar about it, but as he was frowning, wondering about it, a large aircraft appeared low overhead.

"It's a German aircraft!" yelled one of the men. L/Cpl Harrison grabbed his rifle, snapping at the men, "Shoot the bugger!"

Three of the men shot at the aircraft and the pilot turned slightly off his bombing run, but dropped two bombs near the locomotive. They didn't appear to do any damage, but the driver leaned slowly out of his cab and slipped to the ground, bleeding profusely. George raced over to help but two medical orderlies were already there. He stopped at the engine with sudden recognition: it was a Great Western Dean Goods 0-6-0! He had heard that the railways had been asked to provide some locomotives for war work, but he hadn't expected to see any he was familiar with.

Lt Bridewell appeared again. "Lance Corporal Harrison!" he called. "Get the men into the train; we've been called back to the front urgently. There's been another attack and we're needed!"

"Sir, the train driver's injured! What do we do?"

"Get another driver!" shouted Lt Bridewell, hurrying up, "get the train moving!"

"How do we do that, Sir?" asked L/Cpl Harrison.

"I don't bloody know – use your head, Lance Corporal!" the lieutenant was worried about failing to get his men to the front as he had been ordered.

"Useless bastard!" muttered one of the soldiers. "Officers are supposed to lead, not panic."

George climbed into the cab of the engine and saw the French fireman sitting on the cab floor, cradling his bloody right hand. George leaned out of the cab and called to L/Cpl Harrison, "I can drive this, Lance Corporal" he said, "I'm a GWR fireman."

"Good for you, Denton, let's get the train moving again before that stupid bugg-, er, before Lieutenant Bridewell gets any more excited."

Once the men were all aboard the train, L/Cpl Harrison joined him in the cab. "Ready for the off." George gingerly released the handbrake and lifted the regulator. The locomotive began to move and when it was running steadily, he looked into the firebox. "Hmm, needs a bit more coal."

"I'll shovel some in," said L/Cpl Harrison, grabbing the shovel and filling it with coal from the bunker. He was about to throw the coal in when the fireman stopped him, peered into the firebox, and pointed to the right. Harrison threw the coal to where he was shown and their engine responded willingly.

George looked at Harrison shovelling the coal into the firebox and grinned, "We'll make an engineman out of you yet, Corp!"

The journey to the front was uneventful; although the fireman spoke no English, he was able to direct the firing and warn George of the signals. They moved slowly and carefully forward and after two hours reached their detraining point, for the men to be loaded onto lorries and taken to within a couple of miles of the front.

They arrived at their trenches to find a furious major waiting for them.

"Why the hell are you late, Bridewell?" he roared. "We needed your troops here an hour ago."

"Bombs landed near the train, Sir; the driver was injured and I had to organise a replacement crew."

"I see," nodded the Major, mollified, "well, get your men into the trenches, quick as you can."

"Lissen t' the sod," whispered one of the soldiers, "'I 'ad to organise a replacement crew'! – 'e was shittin' isself! It were Denton and 'Arrison wot got us 'ere, not 'im!"

"Quiet in the ranks!" Harrison's voice had no bite in it.

Five weeks later, it appeared that the new troops had taken the Lance Corporal's words to heart as there were relatively few losses. After one particularly vigorous action, in which a heavy German attack was repulsed with the capture of five enemy soldiers, L/Cpl Harrison was promoted to Corporal, and George - who had actually captured three of the men and been seen by the Major to do so - was promoted to Acting Lance Corporal. Nevertheless, success was only temporary, as the Germans set up a machine gun nest some 300 yards away and constantly harassed their sector. Lt Bridewell received a message from the Major to try and deal with it, but the nest was extremely well sited and his men were unable to get close enough for grenades to be lobbed over. Cpl Harrison was ordered to take a night patrol out to try and destroy the nest, but neither he nor his three men returned.

The following two nights, Bridewell sent out more patrols, which also failed to return. On the fourth night, the lieutenant called George over and ordered him to take out another night patrol with three more men, to see what could be done.

"Sir?" said George, "we've lost twelve men already. Perhaps we should try something different? What if I take out two men with grenades on the right and another two men could sneak out over on the left to make a bit of noise and distract-?"

"Are you refusing to obey an order in the face of the enemy, Lance Corporal?" snarled Bridewell.

"Of course not, Sir, I was just thinking that there might be a better meth-"

"Denton, you're only Acting Lance Corporal! It's the officers' job to think! Now get your men out there and deal with that nest!"

"Sir!" George saluted and collected his men. He had them blacken their faces with boot polish, ready to move out. It was two hours before the men in the trench heard a sudden flurry of firing and grenades bursting. Just before dawn, a hoarse call from in front of the trench warned the waiting soldiers not to fire. George, his leg bleeding profusely, and holding on to one of his men, dropped thankfully into the trench.

"They were waiting for us again, Sir," said George. "We lost two men."

Lt Bridewell stared at him. "I don't know why the Major promoted you to Lance Corporal, Denton! I'll have that stripe off you!"

A distant voice came from the trench, "It's not 'im wot's useless, yer bugger, it's you!"

Bridewell's face turned purple in fury. "Who said that?" he yelled. "That's a court martial offence! Who was it?"

But nobody responded.

Two days later, Major Simpson appeared. "Mr Bridewell, any luck with that enemy machine gun nest?"

"I sent patrols out, Sir, over four nights, but we haven't been able to silence it."

"Well, I'll have to call upon the artillery boys. No matter, as long as you haven't lost any men."

"Erm- well, Sir, we did lose some."

"*Some?* How many?"

"Fifteen men did not return from the patrols, Sir."

"*Fifteen of your men?* Good God, man, don't you ever bloody listen to your orders?" The Major was horrified, "I gave you clear instructions *not* to take undue risks with your men!"

"But Sir, one of my men refused to obey an order!" The lieutenant was quick to deflect the negative attention coming his way.

"Refused to obey an order? Who?"

"Acting Lance Corporal Denton, Sir."

Major Simpson paused and turned in shock. "Denton? The man I promoted?"

"Yes Sir!"

"Where is he?"

"He was wounded, Sir. He's here at the First Aid post."

"He could face the firing squad!"

"I believe so, Sir."

"There'll have to be a court martial."

"A court martial, Sir?" Lt Bridewell asked uneasily.

"Of course! We can't just shoot the man, Bridewell!"

But further discussion was cut off as German soldiers suddenly appeared out of their trenches in an attack. The unit grabbed their rifles, leapt up to the firing steps, and began to fire back; on the left, a British heavy machine gun began to chatter and the German advance faltered.

"Counter-attack!" yelled the Major from on top of the trench as the men fixed their bayonets and began to climb over the lip. Major Simpson paused before moving out, looking for Lt Bridewell, who had disappeared. George, a bandage round his leg, was already yards ahead with five men, firing and heading for the machine gun nest. Lt Bridewell appeared again from a dugout, loading his pistol.

"Get out after your men, Bridewell, for God's sake!" Major Simpson was enraged. "You're supposed to damn well lead them, man, not lag behind!"

"Sir!" said Bridewell; he glanced at the major, reluctantly mounted the side of the trench, and moved forward. He did not return from the counter attack.

At the subsequent inquiry, the court martial found Acting Lance Corporal Denton innocent of the charge of failing to obey an order. The Lieutenant Colonel looked at Major Simpson; "I think we might leave it at that, making no further fuss about Bridewell's death; what's your view, Harry?"

"I completely agree, Sir."

The Lt Colonel nodded. "Good, we'll do that," and he turned to

Regimental Sergeant Major; "Your opinion, Sarn't Major? You've seen Lance Corporal Denton in action." The RSM was silent for a moment or two and then replied, "With respect Sir, I'd rather see him as a full Corporal. I reckon he's saved a fair few lives while he's been with us; and the men all respect him." The Lt Col glanced at Major Simpson, who gave a slight nod of agreement.

"Hmm, yes RSM, on reflection I think you're right." He made some notes in a ledger and then looked up. "Congratulations, Corporal Denton. Get your second stripe up and you can start earning it right away."

"Thank you, Sir." George saluted, about-turned, and marched out of the room.

Lt Bridewell was recorded as having been 'killed in action during an attack on German lines'. No mention was made of the discovery that when his body was recovered, it was found with a British Army issue .303 bullet in the head.

Bridewell's replacement was another young lieutenant who, on arriving to take over, sat down beside George and said breezily, "Right ho, Corporal, you've been here longer than I have, let's have your advice."

A soldier sitting in the trench nearby leaned over to nudge his mate and muttered, "Thank God for that; with this one in charge, we might live a bit longer!"

11 - A sad homecoming (March 1919)

In March 1919, the troops were already being repatriated and were issued with demobilisation documents and rail passes to their home towns. Corporal Denton was surprised to be called in to see the Lieutenant Colonel. As he marched into the regimental office, the orderly sergeant typing at his desk sat back and said with a grin, "Now what have you been up to, George? Most of us just get our papers and are told to piss off."

"No idea, Sarge, what've you heard?"

"Me? Simple sergeant, me." He shook his head, "I've heard nowt, but the colonel's not in a bad mood; you might be lucky! Go on in."

George knocked, marched in, came to attention and snapped a salute. "You called for me, Sir?"

"Yes, I did, Corporal Denton. I have a question for you. Have you decided what you want to do after demobilisation?" George pondered the odd question; most soldiers simply returned – or tried to return - to their old jobs. "I expect to return to the railways, Sir. Why do you ask?"

"As you must be aware, the army will be reducing its size considerably after this war, but it will still need a number of competent and experienced NCOs. I have been looking at your file here, Corporal. Major Simpson made particular mention of your impressive actions in the regrettable affair concerning Lt Bridewell, and that, with my own observations of your subsequent behaviour in this company, leads me to believe that you are the sort of man the army has need of in the future. If you were prepared to sign on to another five years in the army, I would offer you promotion to Sergeant, effective immediately."

This offer rocked George back on his heels; the thought of staying in the army had not entered his head. Nevertheless, it was an interesting idea. "Can I let you know tomorrow, Sir? I need to think about this."

Back in the barracks George pondered the offer; he had once as a boy thought about joining the army. The idea of serving further as a senior NCO in a peacetime army required serious consideration and it kept him awake most of the night until he finally came to a decision.

The next morning at 8am sharp, George presented himself at the Lt Colonel's office. "Thank you, Sir, for your offer. I have given it a great deal of thought, but I would rather get back to railway work; I was a Great Western Fireman and hope one day to make Driver like my old man."

"I have to say, I'm disappointed, Corporal Denton, but I understand your decision. Well, good luck to you!"

"Thank you, Sir."

"One final point; just in case your efforts to get back into railway work are not successful, my offer will still be open to you for six months."

"Thank you again, Sir, I'll bear that in mind."

Three weeks later, wearing one of his old suits, George arrived with his demobilisation papers at Swindon Works. The official looked up his file and read for a few moments. "Well, Mr Denton, I think we can offer you your old job back, but you won't be firing straightaway, or at Chester, I'm afraid, there's no vacancy for a fireman there."

"But I had six years firing!"

"Yes, I am aware of that, but you must see that you've been out of firing for almost three years. While we appreciate the good work you have done in defending the realm, we cannot be certain that you are still a competent Fireman. You will have to work with an experienced driver for a while before you can be allotted the formal duties of Fireman. But I note Bristol's Bath Road is short of firemen and you are familiar with the roads there - and your father works there now. That should help you get back to your previous level more quickly."

"Yessir, I understand; and thank you."

A fortnight later, George was back with the Great Western Railway. He was able to live at home again with his parents and told them of his disappointment.

"Don't blame the Railway, son," said his father, "there have been many changes since you left to go to war."

"What changes, Dad?"

"For one thing, we've had government bureaucrats telling us railwaymen how to run our railway; and the rolling stock hasn't had the attention it needed for years. It's run down and we've been driving engines that are sometimes in poor condition, some even due for scrapping. We don't always get the good Welsh steam coal that we need and the engines don't like the rubbish we're often supplied with. Many of the platelayers joined up and haven't returned so the track is not up to the standard you were used to."

"I'm sure I'll soon get back into the swing of things." But George felt that there was something else that was of concern to his father; he sounded unusually down in the mouth. "Anything else wrong, Dad?"

Henry Denton nodded worriedly. "I'm anxious about your mother," he said, "she's got a bout of the flu, and she's not recovering as well as she normally does. She tells me she's fine, but I don't think she is."

George had wondered about his mother when he had first returned; she had been in bed and hadn't looked at all well, in spite of claiming to be on the mend. Their family doctor was becoming a regular visitor and he too seemed puzzled at her slow recovery. He thought it might be a result of the poor diet that many had had to get used to during the war when the German U-boats had almost brought the country to its knees by cutting off much of the food imports from the Empire. The only advice to George's father was to keep a close eye on his wife and report any deterioration in her condition.

Arriving at Bristol's Bath Road shed, George was welcomed by many of the enginemen whom he had known before, and he felt right at home immediately. The smells of hot oil, burning coal, and steam issuing from locomotives, with cinders under foot along the uneven tracks, smoke drifting across the gloomy interior of the shed; all made a change from the explosions, cries of wounded men and the stink of cordite that he had grown to detest over the last three years. But the conditions at the shed were unsatisfactory and he recalled his father's warning about poor coal and unkempt locomotives. He was also very disturbed to find himself once more paired with Driver Jock McKendrick, who clearly hadn't changed his attitude to those unfortunate enough to be under his authority. George, however, had learned a thing or two in the army and decided he was not going to put up with any more nonsense from McKendrick.

"So, it's Fireman Denton again, eh? Well, don't forget I'm your boss in my cab, and you'll do what you're told."

"Of course I will, Driver McKendrick, as long as it's legal and reasonable."

"No mate, it's simpler than that; you'll bloody well do what I tell you and no argument!"

George stared at his driver but didn't reply.

"Well?" demanded McKendrick.

"Well what?"

"Did you understand what I'm saying?"

"Of course I did," replied George evenly, "no argument, you said; well, I'm not arguing." Ignoring his driver, he carried on checking the gauges. He knew all about dumb insolence from his time in the army, and as an NCO had also learned how to deal with it, but he was fairly sure McKendrick hadn't. He had also learned how to handle bullies, and he wondered how long it was going to be before he would need to bring his driver down to size. It turned out to be sooner than he expected.

Early on in their next shift, they were taking a short, unfitted goods from Westbury to Bath and while George was firing, McKendrick moved over to the firebox to check the fire, carefully timing his move to coincide with George's swing with the shovel full of coal. In trying to avoid McKendrick's legs, the coal spilled all over the cab floor.

"Whoops! That was careless, Fireman Denton! Clean that all up."

Without any comment, George began to shovel up the coal scattered over the cab floor, and then he carefully hosed down the wooden floorboards with the coal-watering pipe. When that was done, he picked a whetstone out of his pocket and started to sharpen the edge of his shovel, which began to take on a razor-like edge.

"What the hell are you doing that for?" McKendrick asked nervously.

"Sharpening my shovel, Driver McKendrick?" George stared grimly at his driver, "Why, it's to make it easier for the shovel to go into the coal – or wherever else it's going. Much better if you keep out of my way when I'm firing. Don't want you to get hurt, do we?" George turned to the tender, seized the coal hammer and smashed it down on a lump of coal too large to go into the firebox. He opened the firebox flap, peered inside, and muttered that the fire needed to be shifted about. He turned, drew out the long pricker from its tunnel in the tender and poked it around in the firebed for a while until he was satisfied with the level of the fire. By this time, the last two feet of the pricker were white hot. He withdrew it from the firebox and swung it round, forcing Driver McKendrick to leap out of the way in the cramped cab before George slid the pricker back into its tunnel.

"Oops! Dangerous places, locomotive cabs," George commented breezily to McKendrick, "have to be extra careful in them; we don't want any nasty accidents."

"Just be bloody careful with that pricker, don't wave it about!" McKendrick's fright was showing.

"It's eight foot long. How else do I get it into and out of the firebox?" George asked reasonably. "I have to rake the fire from time to time."

"I, er-, I er- Just watch it, that's all!"

"Right, Driver McKendrick, I'll watch it," George carried on with his firing unperturbed.

McKendrick was quietly fuming, but didn't know what else he could say, so he kept his mouth shut. He was also becoming wary; this fireman of his was showing more guts than he had before and furthermore, he was handling his steel implements as if they were weapons. He would need careful watching. On the other hand, Fireman Denton was, in spite of his three years' absence from the cab, obviously well on top of his job, and a thought occurred to Driver McKendrick: if Denton were to be encouraged to go for promotion back to full Fireman, perhaps back up north to Wellington shed, then he, McKendrick, would feel a good deal more at ease in his own cab with a younger – and more malleable - fireman. He decided to give his fireman a few driving stints and make appropriate representation to management about Denton's ability. He wasn't worried about whether George was ready for driving; if he wasn't, and caused an accident, that was no concern of Driver McKendrick's.

Initially, George was surprised and pleased at his driver's apparent change of attitude and he took every opportunity to hone his driving skills; even McKendrick was occasionally impressed. Very soon, George was called into the office at Bath Road shed and told that he was to be reinstated as a fully registered Fireman, and a transfer back to his previous shed at Wellington was available if he wished. He did wish, and he moved back up north.

Yet all George's positive feelings were set at nought early one morning when he received a letter from his father, urgently requesting a visit home; his mother was very ill. George arranged leave from his job and arrived home to find his mother critical and his father in despair. She smiled when he came into her room but she had, like so many others, become a victim of the flu epidemic which was sweeping the country and she died three days later. George had been no stranger in the army to the death of those he knew, of course, but this was quite different and George was devastated. Quiet apart from anything else, it seemed so unfair after all the years of war and final victory to lose the mother he loved so deeply.

12 - George meets Alice and an old colleague (September 1922)

"Come on, George, I met this girl in Leicester Square who said if ever I was in London again, she'd give me a right old time, and she had a friend who would do the same for any mate of mine!"

George and his driver Andy Egerton were on Platform Three at Paddington, where they had just got off a local train which had brought them from Old Oak Common shed. Their next duty was not until the following morning, returning north on a Birkenhead express, so they had a free evening. Andy had been instructed to learn the road between Wolverhampton and Paddington and had taken his fireman with him; they had travelled in comfort from Chester to Wolverhampton, where they had joined the crew on the Star class 4-6-0 to Paddington.

George Denton was no prude; he had spent time in Paris on his odd spots of leave during the Great War and he was familiar with the more earthy delights available to relaxed and lustful troops let loose from the trenches. Most of them were intent on emptying their pockets in order to fill their throats with the cheap *vin ordinaire* and, if any coins were left over, these could be handed to ladies who could help them - over half an hour or so - to forget the purgatory they had to return to.

Nevertheless, during the increasing number of driving turns which brought George to Paddington, the London girls only had a superficial appeal and, if the truth be known, he felt that the money they demanded could be better employed earning interest in a bank account, where it could be used for a more worthwhile purpose. He felt that life – since he had been granted it when so many others hadn't - ought to offer rather more than a quick tumble in a none-too-clean bed whenever he visited the capital.

"Er- not for me, Mr Egerton, thanks; I've an aunt in Wimbledon I haven't seen since before the war and she's invited me to tea this evening. I'll see you in the shed tomorrow."

"Your loss, George," admonished his driver. "As you know, next week my regular fireman's back from his leave and you won't get another chance." This did not worry George unduly; he knew that he would soon be on another regular duty to and from the capital.

Aunt Amy and Uncle Jack were a retired couple living in a quiet street in Wimbledon, not too far from the London and South Western Railway main line to Devon and Cornwall. George spent a few minutes watching two of the LSWR expresses as they tore through Wimbledon station at high speed before he turned and continued his way to the home of his elderly relatives.

Family chat took place after the evening meal but was interrupted by a knock at the door. Uncle Jack got up to see to it and a few moments later he ushered a young lady into the room. "Alice, meet our nephew, George. George, this is Alice Newton, our neighbour's daughter. She needs the help of a strong man to help her father move a couch. Would you mind-?"

"Of course, I'd be happy to assist." George rather liked the look of Alice and was only too pleased to have an excuse to talk to her. Alice proved to be vivacious and interesting, and George quickly decided that he ought to try and cultivate a closer relationship to these elderly relatives whom he had rather neglected since his younger days. He could now expect occasional firing trips to London so could easily squeeze in a Wimbledon visit now and then and who knew – perhaps Alice could be enticed to look in if he were visiting.

Major changes were being discussed in the railway world; the London and North Western and the Lancashire and Yorkshire had amalgamated to form by far the largest railway company in the world, and the government was planning to combine all the remaining companies into four larger groups. This naturally gave rise to major insecurities amongst most railwaymen at every level, who were wondering about their jobs. At the top ranks in these dozens of companies, men were also wondering who would be taking the reins of the big four. Great Western enginemen had just lost their beloved Chief Mechanical Engineer: Mr Churchward had retired, and his deputy, Mr Collett, had taken over at Swindon. It was a source of comfort that he was known to be likely to hold his predecessor's views in engine design. In any case, most of them believed they already had the finest fleet in the country thanks to Mr Churchward's innovative rule.

Safety had also long been an issue but the Great Western had already had a decade of experience of their Automatic Train Control system, which gave an audible warning to a driver if he passed a signal at 'danger'; this had proved itself to be highly reliable and was being implemented widely across the system. It had not prevented all accidents, but the GWR safety record was nevertheless enviable.

George was by now a Passed Fireman and allowed to drive under certain circumstances, but the ATC did not solve all problems, as George found out one day with Driver Reg Bilsom on a 2-6-0 Mogul Birmingham to Birkenhead semi-fast passenger. As they were speeding towards the platform at Codsall, he saw a driver jump down from a 4-6-0 Saint class express locomotive waiting on the up platform and begin to walk across the track of the down platform through which they were passing. The Saint driver did not appear to have seen them and they had no hope at all of stopping in time. Reg blew the whistle frantically and as they raced past the waiting Saint, they saw the driver fall back. Both George and his driver were deeply shocked; they could not stop so continued on to Wellington.

"Did we hit him?" asked George, agonised as they drove past the station.

"Don't know!" said Reg, equally upset. "I saw him fall, but whether we hit him or not, I couldn't say!"

At Wellington there was no report of any injuries to employees, but it was possible that the news hadn't filtered through yet so they tried to find out at Shrewsbury. Yet here again, no report of any incident had been recorded. During the next hour-and-a-half, both George and Reg were very subdued at the thought of what they might have done and, arriving at Chester for a break in their shift, they tried once again to discover whether they had killed a colleague. But Control at Chester had no knowledge of any fatality.

Their return journey had them taking a big Star class 4-6-0 on a Paddington express as far as Birmingham, where they were to come off their shift. In the shed the talk was of the problems they might have dealing with ancient Cambrian Railway engines after the big amalgamation, now planned for the following year. Nobody mentioned anything about employees' injuries or deaths in the system. Both enginemen were relieved; had anyone been killed, the word would have gone round the shed like greased lightning.

One day in Hereford it was raining hard and in the enginemen's cabin crewmen were relaxing over their tea when George and his driver walked in. They had just sat down to wait for the return to Wellington on the cushions when the door opened once more and a familiar figure entered; it was Driver Jock McKendrick. He spotted George instantly and came over.

"So, Fireman Denton; I hear the unfortunate northern shed has been lumbered with you again."

George wasn't accepting any more nonsense from this man. "Driver McKendrick," he said pleasantly, "there's a vacant seat in that corner right over on the far side. Why don't you take your tea there then we'll all be happier."

McKendrick grunted but took his tea away.

"What was that all about?" asked Reg in surprise.

"He was my driver for a while in Bristol and the main reason I asked for a transfer. He's a nasty piece of work and I feel sorry for any fireman unlucky enough to have him as a driver."

"Bad as that?"

"Actually, he's quite a good driver, but all the firemen detest him."

At that moment, the shedmaster came in, looked around, then curled his finger, indicating that McKendrick should come into his office. Ten minutes later, the driver returned to the cabin, stalked over to George with a smirk on his face and said, "Bit of good luck for you, Denton; you're firing to a proper driver on a fast freight to Bristol."

"What on earth are you talking about?"

"Fireman Rawlings has been taken ill and I need a replacement so since you're set to return on the cushions, you're obviously available as a spare fireman."

"But-?"

"Don't worry; it's all been checked with Control and they've agreed. You'll get a longer trip on the cushions from Bristol! Come on!"

McKendrick turned to walk out but felt his shoulder held firmly. He turned back to find an angry Reg Bilsom standing facing him. "You'd be wise to get out before you get your face smacked by another 'proper' driver; now you can piss off!"

McKendrick backed off and, without a word, turned and stomped out with George following. They climbed into the cab of their 2-6-0 Mogul where Fireman Rawlings was waiting. He was very pale but claimed he wanted to stay in the cab.

"Up to you!" grunted McKendrick, without interest.

George did a quick check of the cab, including the fire and water gauges, and they moved off and collected their train. The run was uneventful until they were approaching Leominster, where a rough patch of track had George spill some coal he was shovelling into the firebox.

"See, and I heard you were a good fireman!" taunted McKendrick.

George ignored him and cleaned up the coal. McKendrick looked at Fireman Rawlings sitting on the seat, watching. "What d'you think of a fireman who spills coal all the time?"

George took the coal watering pipe to spray the coal in the tender; as he turned it on, some water splashed McKendrick's legs.

"Look what you're doing, you clumsy idiot!" yelled McKendrick.

"Sorry!" smiled George, then he glanced out of the cab. "We've got the distant against us."

"Never mind the bloody distant!" shouted McKendrick furiously, "Just watch yourself in my cab!" He began to wipe his legs, leaving the regulator wide open.

Moments later George, looking out of the cab, said, "We've got the home at danger too."

"For God's sake just do your job properly and keep my cab clean!" McKendrick's temper hadn't improved at all. He did not lower the regulator, and without thinking, he cancelled the ATC warning in his cab until both George and Dick Rawlings shouted "Stop!" McKendrick yanked the regulator down and slammed on the engine brakes but it was too late; they had overrun the signal by about 200 yards. Fortunately, there was nothing immediately in their path. Driver McKendrick was silent for the rest of the trip and George left them at Bristol yard with only a brief word to Fireman Rawlings.

At the subsequent enquiry held in Swindon, all three men were called in to explain the offence. The supervisor addressed his concluding remarks to Driver McKendrick. "A signal passed at danger is an extremely serious offence and you ignored two warnings by your firemen, and even cancelled the ATC alarm in the cab. You were exceedingly fortunate that no-one was hurt. The Great Western cannot accept such inexcusable action on the part of one of its drivers. You are hereby dismissed from the company."

Both firemen were exonerated. Dick Rawlings was ecstatic. "Bath Road firemen will be delighted," he chortled, "best news we've had this year!"

George, while he had no sympathy for Jock McKendrick, was not so happy. "Pity it had to come to this," he commented, "it's a waste of a good driver. Someone in authority should have spoken to McKendrick long ago."

13 - George and Alice (July 1924)

The railway grouping of the previous year had begun to settle down and the three new companies: the London, Midland and Scottish Railway; the London and North Eastern Railway, and the Southern Railway, were busy establishing their individual identities. The GWR alone was the only one to have retained its identity and was gradually imposing its methods and ideas on its new Welsh constituents. However, George, normally very interested in the practices and politics of the railways, was distracted; he and his young lady were to be married after a short courtship. George was now 34 and felt that he had missed out on this aspect of life that most younger men were already enjoying.

The only disappointment for George was that his mother was not there to see him marry Alice. He knew she would have strongly approved of his choice of bride; his father was overjoyed, and his pleasure in his son's marriage went some way to making up for the sadness that had been part of his life since he had lost his wife five years earlier. Life had never been the same for Henry and he had decided that the year his son got married would also be the one when he left the railways.

Although neither George nor Alice had strong religious beliefs, they both felt that a traditional church wedding would suit them. The minister in the little church in Wellington also suspected that he would see very little of them in his church, but nevertheless agreed to marry them. The wedding was quiet and simple but Alice's parents felt that their daughter was in very good hands, even if she would now be living apart from them and most likely only see them at infrequent intervals.

George and his new bride caught an evening train to Shrewsbury, where they picked up a Birkenhead express and were in Chester and their honeymoon hotel in time for a late supper. They planned to spend the next week exploring this historical city with its Roman heritage. George had developed a fondness for the place before his army days.

In their entrance to the hotel bedroom, Alice was rather tense; she knew George was older than most of the young men who had shown interest in her, and she accepted that he had experience in such matters. He had, after all, been to Paris, which, as all English girls knew, was the fount of sinful pleasure.

As they lay in bed the following morning, Alice glanced at the bedside clock and immediately wriggled out of bed. "It's already eight o'clock, George!" she exclaimed, shocked. "What *will* the other hotel guests be thinking!"

George knew exactly what the male guests, at least, would be thinking. "They'll be envying us, my love," he said, amused at her obvious embarrassment.

They took their breakfast and left the hotel for their first full day out as a married couple. The Queen Hotel was next to Francis Thompson's masterpiece, the General Station, and they took a tram to the centre of the city where Alice delighted in exploring the shops in the Rows, the curious two-level sets of shops leading out from the Cross in four directions, based on the plan of the old

Roman camp. The city had been the main Roman military base for north-west Britannia and its modern centre, contained within the complete set of medieval walls (which had held off Cromwell's Roundheads until the Battle of Rowton Heath), still largely followed the Roman plan, albeit with Anglo-Saxon extensions.

George left Alice to her shopping for an hour while he went to explore the other station in the city. This was the LNER Northgate station, part of the semi-independent Cheshire Lines Committee railway - a curious misnomer, as most of the network was in Lancashire and the company headquarters were in Liverpool Central station. The CLC and the Somerset and Dorset Joint Railway were the only two sizeable companies which had not been incorporated into the 'Big Four'. The CLC was associated with the LNER and used its stock, whereas the S&D used a combination of LMS and Southern stock.

Northgate station was, unlike Chester General, a small terminus and served only two routes: Manchester via Northwich, and the Wrexham run. But it was only a small, four-track terminus with two platforms. Its overall roof was of utilitarian design, confirming its lowly status compared with Manchester or Liverpool Central stations. Nevertheless, passengers liked their arrival at Northgate because it gave them a mere five-minute walk to the Market Square, whereas Chester General was far less conveniently sited and one needed a tram or bus ride to reach the centre.

Oddly, there was another station at Liverpool Road, less than half a mile from Northgate on the Wrexham line, which boasted four well-laid-out platforms. This had been built by the Great Central, perhaps to allow future Manchester to Birkenhead passenger services to stop in Chester, bypassing the Northgate terminus, but this service never began, and even on race days the specials from the LNER still terminated at Northgate. Consequently, the station rarely saw passengers, for the whole of its existence.

Meeting up again with Alice in the Market Square, George took her for their morning coffee in the up-market Blossoms Hotel. George winced when he saw the bill and made a private resolution to avoid such places in future; as a fireman, his wages didn't allow for expenditure of this nature. Their honeymoon at the Queen Hotel had already taken a very large chunk out of his savings and he wanted at a later date to be able to afford to buy a house.

They took an evening circuit around the City Walls, pausing at the Northgate Bridge to admire the sunset over the Welsh hills and to ponder the moods of the king's soldiers manning their cannon on Morgan's Mount on the north-facing wall.

A bus trip to the nearby Welsh hills allowed them to walk to the top of Moel Vammaeu, where they met a local who informed them that there had been peace between the Welsh and English in that part of the world for many centuries, but that in King Edward's time things were very different. 'There's many a yew bow in Chester' had been a Welsh saying, referring to the frequent attacks from the English stronghold of Chester. The man told them that when the king had given his first son to the Welsh as their prince, he had also granted him two other significant titles.

"Well, yes," said George, "it's common knowledge that he's the Prince of Wales and the Duke of Cornwall."

"Ah, but did you know that he is also the Earl of Chester?"

"Is that right?" George was surprised.

"Chester is a County Palatine; such counties had a degree of independence and were set up to give their earls a position from which they could defend the country against depredations from the Scots and us Welsh."

The next day, George puzzled Alice by announcing that they would be having an 'overhead and underground' day. They took a train to Birkenhead Woodside for a ferry trip across the Mersey to Liverpool; here, George took Alice for a ride on the Liverpool Overhead Railway, where she could see how busy the docks were from the train running on piers above. The double-track electric railway ran several miles from Dingle in the east to Seaforth in the west of Liverpool's docklands and had been built to give the dock workers rapid access to their place of work.

"Right, now my love, we go underground," said George, and he took her to the nearest underground station to return to Birkenhead via the Mersey Railway under the river.

All too soon, George was back at work, but welcome news awaited his arrival. He was to face his driver's examination in a month's time. Alice was kept busy organising their rented house while George once more took up studying the drivers' rule book with deep concentration, in preparation for his test. The physical exam was no trouble for him; like most firemen, he was as fit as a fiddle. Shovelling tonnes of coal on a daily basis did not allow for any extension around a man's waist. The written exam and the actual test on the road with an inspector did not give him any serious difficulty either, and he passed with flying colours.

George's first regular duty was an all-stations Wellington to Crewe on an unfitted goods schedule. His fireman, Josh Simpson, was an elderly ex-driver who had had been involved in a serious accident some years previously and had rather lost his nerve, but was quite prepared to go back to firing so long as he didn't have any responsibility for driving. When he heard about Josh firing to George, Len Baxendale said that Josh had very little to say for himself, but was highly reliable; he had been an excellent driver until the accident, for which he hadn't been responsible.

"Josh keeps his gob shut for the whole shift, usually, but if he does say owt, then listen - it'll be worth it."

George's regular run was to travel to Wolverhampton, pick up their train from Banbury - normally hauled by a 2-6-0 Mogul - and take it to Crewe to hand over to an LMS engine, before taking their Mogul to Gresty Lane GWR shed for turning and servicing. Later, they would return to Wolverhampton with another southbound goods. The shift did not cover many miles but as an unfitted freight they had to give way to nearly every other train on this busy route; they spent many an hour waiting in sidings for more important traffic to pass through.

The waiting gave George an opportunity to try and draw Josh into conversation. This proved rather more difficult than George had anticipated as Josh was in the habit of nodding gently rather than replying to George's attempts to converse. For the first fortnight, George, who although not unduly garrulous himself, did enjoy the occasional chat whilst waiting at signal or in sidings, found this very heavy-going.

In the third week they were requested, due to an LMS crew

shortage, to take a local passenger to Stafford. Waiting in the up bay platform at Wellington, Josh leaned over to George and said, "Ye'll have to give 'er a bit o' stick 'ere to git away from the bay; more'n one driver's 'ad ter stop and ease back ter take a run up the 'ill."

George nodded. "Thanks for that, Josh." As soon as they got the right away, George pushed the regulator higher than he would normally have done and they moved away smartly with their seven non-corridors, breasting the rise with little to spare. Once well on their way, George looked at Josh and said, "Thanks again, Josh. I would have embarrassed myself without your advice. That grade is steeper than it looks." Josh simply nodded and went back to his firing.

Over the next few months, George's friendly personality seemed to overcome some of Josh's taciturn manner. While the latter never became talkative, he did partake in intermittent conversations and George was able to glean a great many useful tips from the ex-driver. George felt considerable regret when, some months later, they finally parted.

Driving south from Crewe one evening a week before he left, George had an idea. He glanced out of the cab side of the Stella class 2-4-0 and exclaimed in apparent pain. "Josh, can you take the regulator for a spell?" he called to his fireman, "I've got a smut in my eye and can't see well. I'll have to remove it!"

Josh hesitated, then said, "Aye, I'll tak' 'er," and seized the regulator.

George pulled out his handkerchief and took his time dabbing at his eye, pausing occasionally to see to the fire - one eye closed - before grabbing his handkerchief once more. Meanwhile, they stopped at Nantwich and Market Drayton. Eventually he grunted, "Got it!" He pushed his handkerchief back into his pocket and took over the regulator once more.

"Why don't you get back on this side of the cab, Josh?" he asked. "There's nothing wrong with your driving!"

Josh nodded, a slow smile spreading over his face. "Aye, I might at that," he said, "'an there were nowt wrong wi' your eye, neither!"

14 - George gets two birthday presents (July 1925)

George and Alice were in London on holiday. They had viewed Buckingham Palace, visited Kensington Gardens, Hyde Park with the Albert Memorial, and the Tower of London. George had traipsed through umpteen clothes and shoe shops without complaint, but as they caught a tram down Knightsbridge, Alice said suddenly, "Let's get off here, there's something we need." George sighed quietly. *How many clothes or shoes does a female actually need?* He wasn't foolish enough to ask out loud. Although only recently married, he already knew the futility – not to mention hazard - of such a question.

They entered a large department store and George noted the name 'Harrods' above the entrance. Even he had heard of this famous shop, so he did not begrudge his wife the chance to at least investigate.

"What exactly are you looking for here?" George asked nervously; he had also heard that the prices in Harrods were not what they were used to at home, where costs were more closely in line with wages such as his.

"It's your birthday soon, my love," Alice replied as they sauntered through ladies' undergarments.

"Not sure I need a brassiere," muttered George, looking around.

"Just for that," said Alice, "I've a good mind to have you measured for one!"

They walked on with Alice gazing round. "I saw something in a shop the other day which I am sure you will like," she said.

George's nerves returned; he didn't like the sound of this in Harrods. But his fears turned out to be unfounded; Alice caught sight of a formally dressed salesman and approached him. "Do you sell toy trains?"

The salesman smiled at her. "Certainly we do, madam. How old is the little lad?"

Alice glanced at George, and, smiling sweetly at the sales assistant, replied, "35!"

As they left the assistant, George nudged her. "When we get back to our hotel bedroom, Mrs Denton, you are going to pay for that!"

Alice's eyes widened and her eyebrows rose; there was a suggestion of a smile on her face. "Ooh, goody!" she breathed, as they proceeded to the toy department. Here she bought George one of the new Basset-Lowke brand trains and some track.

Later over tea and scones, George asked, "Anyway, how did you know I wanted a model railway?"

"Last week we were to meet at our cake shop and you were 20 minutes late," she began.

"I was held up on my shift!" interrupted George.

"No you weren't," replied Alice firmly, "you could have been on time. I watched you from across the road as you stared into the toyshop window for a quarter of an hour. I went over later to see what you had been staring at." She paused. "There is another matter. I've been waiting to tell you. The doctor yesterday confirmed it. We are to have a child."

George stared at her. "A child?"

"Yes, you know; one of those small, noisy creatures that run around the house and generally make a nuisance of themselves."

"I'll be a father!" George said after a stunned pause, shaking his head in wonder.

"My, George, you *are* quick off the mark."

But fatherhood was not the only major change in George's life that year; he was offered a position as Driver back south at Bristol's St Philip's Marsh shed and accepted with alacrity. He and Alice moved to a small village outside the city and put the money down for a little house on the outskirts of the village, from which George had only a half-mile walk to the station; from there was a fairly good train service to Temple Meads. As a new driver, he was placed in a shunting link to begin with and began to work his way up the links, but it wasn't long before his ability was recognised by the powers-that-be.

Bristol was a far busier railway centre than Wellington and was, indeed, the original home of the GWR. It was Bristol merchants who promoted the railway to London, and the Great Western began life in 1835 using Brunel's broad gauge of seven-foot-half-an-inch as its standard. Throughout most of the nineteenth century, the GWR maintained its broad gauge from Paddington north-west to Wolverhampton, west to South Wales and to the West Country as far as Penzance. The GWR had claimed (with some justification) that its gauge was more efficient than Stephenson's accepted standard of four-foot-eight-and-a-half inches, which most of the kingdom's other railways had adopted. It was in fact 1892 before the last broad gauge train ran from Paddington, and over one remarkable weekend in May the whole of the main line west of Plymouth was finally converted to standard gauge. As a civil engineer, Brunel gave the GWR an excellent series of accomplishments, although his early steam locomotives left a great deal to be desired, requiring much correction. Even then, they were quickly abandoned in favour of his assistant Gooch's far superior designs.

One of George's first runs as a driver gave him a serious fright as well as a boost in confidence. He was taking a train of 30 empty coal wagons back to a South Wales colliery and was climbing slowly up a short grade when a coupling between two wagons broke. Released suddenly from half its load, his Mogul 2-6-0 locomotive began to pick up speed. George instantly sounded the emergency code on the whistle to warn the guard that the train had parted. The guard in turn applied his brake to try and hold the rear of the train on the grade. Since the train was not vacuum fitted, as soon as he had halted his part of the train, George told his fireman to drop off, run back, and try and pin down the hand brake on each wagon in the rear half of the train to assist the guard in preventing it slipping backwards; the engine brake was sufficient to hold the front half. This copybook regulation procedure enabled the fireman and the guard to prevent a runaway and possible serious crash.

The guard then ran back down the line and placed detonators to warn any oncoming driver of the obstruction ahead. George sent his fireman once more ahead to go to the next signal box and inform the bobby of what had happened. The bobby would phone the signalman in the preceding box to stop anything from following.

George's rapid reaction saved a potentially serious incident and enhanced his reputation among his Bristol colleagues. Several of them knew the fright of having an unfitted goods train part, and they were highly appreciative of the action of such a new driver to a difficult situation. He was already a source of gossip on account of his constantly clean and tidy appearance, even after a full shift in the cab.

Bristol's St Philip's Marsh shed was a large one, handling mostly freight traffic with an allocation of almost 90 locomotives and over 200 crewmen, nearly half of them drivers. Already, George was coming to the attention of senior men. Not surprisingly, he began relatively quickly to work his way through the links. He was also popular among his colleagues as he did not let his undoubted ability go to his head. He made no secret of his view that a lowly unfitted goods train was much harder to drive than the express passenger trains to which most drivers aspired; it required considerably more attention and competence. This view did not sit well with a few top link drivers, who regarded themselves as the pinnacle of their profession; however, most experienced drivers knew he was right, even if they were reluctant to admit it. Express drivers were generally concerned about accurate timekeeping, and controlling the train was not usually a major problem with continuous vacuum brakes.

Handling the train itself was not always the sole concern of the cab crew; at country stations, there could be a very wide variety of goods to be handled and sometimes crewmen needed to give the station staff a hand. Moreover, the fireman, not the driver, was in charge of shunting operations once the engine left the running lines. The railways were by law forbidden from refusing to carry general goods, regardless of the profitability (road carriers were exempt from this regulation). This was especially true of any animals consigned on passenger trains and they had to be placed in the guard's compartment. Normally, the guard and porters could deal with such traffic, but occasionally the footplatemen came to help.

One day George had to use his initiative to help the passenger guard with a large and distinctly unfriendly Alsatian; the dog had somehow got its leash loose of a wall bar in the guard's compartment and wouldn't allow the man back into his coach after he had stepped out to wave his green flag. The guard slammed the door on the dog to keep it inside while he shouted for help. George walked along the platform to find out what the difficulty was. The guard explained.

George said, "Stand by ready to open your door when I give the word." He picked up a nearby fire bucket and walked back to the door. "Open up," he called.

The guard opened the door and the dog leaped forward, snarling, to receive a bucketful of cold water in its face. It backed off in shock and the guard grabbed its leash and refastened it to the bar, well away from his seat. "Keep another bucket of cold water handy," advised George, "and if it gets angry, flick a cupful in its face. It'll soon calm down."

"I should've thought of that," nodded the guard. "Ta for the idea."

George's reputation for a tidy appearance took a bad knock one day. He had a 28 class 2-8-0 heavy goods locomotive with a long, loaded coal train to Didcot, where an Old Oak Common crew would take over for the remaining stretch to London. They had pulled into a siding at Didcot to detach several coal wagons for the shed there, and for the Old Oak crew to board. As George and his fireman walked past their trucks to the enginemen's cabin for their break and lunch, George noticed that the right-hand locking bar on the wagon door was loose.

"Better fix that before it comes undone on the road somewhere and tips its load onto the track," he said. But he hadn't noticed that his fireman had already seen the problem and was lifting the left-hand bar on the same door to drop it back firmly into its hole. At the moment when both locking bars had been released, the weight of the coal behind the door forced it open and both enginemen instantly leaped aside to avoid injury. Neither was hurt but they were covered in coal dust from head to toe. Two nearby shunters came over to help but then stopped, helpless with laughter at the sight of the two blackened enginemen. The coal was soon shovelled back into the wagon and George and his fireman received a reprimand from the yardmaster; but the reprimand had no bite in it as he was trying hard not to chuckle while he administered it.

They managed a superficial clean before returning to Bristol shed, agreeing to make no mention of the incident to their mates; the ribbing they would get didn't bear thinking about and they needed time to be ready to deal with it.

"Hey coal merchants!" shouted an engineman as they came in to book off. "The boss wants a word with yer!"

It seemed the word had already spread.

15 – Variety is the spice of life (May 1926)

Railwaymen had finally had enough – the working classes had generally believed that the 'War to end all wars' (as the Great War was sometimes described) would lead to a change of heart in governments and a fairer deal for the workers who had, after all, done most of the actual fighting and suffering. But in the area of management and the concomitant matter of wages, very little had changed. Indeed, there were moves to reduce wages in order to combat the economic downturn which had occurred. Workers were beginning to see that unless serious action was taken, the issues would probably not be dealt with. The Trade Union Congress called a general strike and miners, transport workers and many others joined it, threatening to damage the country's economy even further.

George was not intending to join the strike, being generally a law-abiding man, but a week before it began, an incident with a passenger made him change his mind. He was returning with a local passenger train from Swindon to Temple Meads and stopped at Wootton Bassett, where an elderly and obviously angry gentleman stomped up to the cab. "Are you one of these misguided drivers who are going to strike to defend the treacherous coal miners?" he demanded.

"I hadn't intended to strike, sir," replied George, "but the strike may not go ahead anyway. The government might reconsider the miners' conditions."

"Reconsider?" the man snapped. "Why should the government

reconsider? We can't afford to continue to pay miners what they want. We all have to assist the government and tighten our belts; I employ fourteen workers in my business and they are all going to have to take a pay cut."

"And you too, sir? Are you going to reduce your salary by a third, like the miners may have to?"

"Me? Good heavens! I'm an employer; why should I reduce my salary?"

"I see, sir, you don't feel that you too should assist the government and tighten your belt? Have I got that right?"

The gentleman's eyebrows shot up in indignation. "You are an insolent young man, and I shall be writing to Great Western Railway management, you can be sure of that!" He strode furiously away.

"After that, I think I shall also join any bloody strike!" said George's fireman.

"Yes," said George, nodding, "I think I will, too."

The country's railway system was almost completely crippled, although a few railwaymen continued to work, and there were many volunteers who helped man the trains so consequently a few still ran. A number of retired railwaymen returned to help do the jobs which needed professional expertise. It was hardly surprising to see a good many female volunteers assisting; women had confirmed during the Great War that they were actually perfectly able to do what had hitherto been considered 'men's work'. They assisted with ticket collecting, passenger management (at this they often proved to be better than men), and were noted even doing heavy work as porters. On rare occasions, they had even been spotted in locomotive cabs but the authorities immediately evicted them when this was observed.

The strike lasted for just over a week. However, George did not join any of the more aggressive workers who tried to prevent the volunteers and non-striking railwaymen from doing their work, and when some went so far as to derail the *Flying Scotsman* train, George immediately re-joined the workforce, angry at the callous attempt to cause injury to innocent passengers. Striking, he believed, was quite justified under the circumstances, but actively causing danger was emphatically not.

The railway unions were clearly getting nowhere with the government and many men began to return to work in order not to lose pay. Waiting one morning at Temple Meads with a local train from Bristol to Portishead, George saw that the ticket collector talking to the guard was female. He sauntered over to introduce himself.

"Ah, George," said the guard, "meet our ticket collector, Lady Wilberforce. Her husband runs a horse racing stable somewhere up near Stroud."

"Pleased to meet you, my Lady," replied George, surprised to learn that the 'quality' were getting involved in volunteer work.

Lady Wilberforce smiled pleasantly, "Constance, please, Driver, 'my Lady' sounds so terribly formal and I'm sure you're not such a formal man?"

"Driver George Denton," answered George with a returning smile. "I don't know about being a formal man; I just do my job to the best of my ability."

The guard commented, "He's being modest, Constance, he's

already one of the best drivers in our shed."

"Oh I am pleased," replied Constance, "I was telling David only last week that if there was a strike, I should love to work on a train. Ladies in my position so rarely get to do anything really useful!"

"David?" queried George.

"Oh, the Prince of Wales, dear; he was visiting Sir Henry's stables in order to find out which horse to put some of his money on."

"And did you give him a name?"

She laughed heartily, "Oh no! I told him he should watch and decide for himself; if I gave him the name and the horse fell over, he would never let me forget it."

George glanced at the platform clock. "Well, you must please excuse me, your La- er, Constance, we'll be leaving in three minutes. I must get back to the cab."

As he was accelerating out of the station, George told fireman Danny Butler how the ticket collector on their train that day was a member of the nobility; and although she associated with the very highest of society, was not afraid to chatter with the hoi polloi.

At the end of the strike, George saw Lady Wilberforce once more as she left the platform for the last time, giving him a cheery wave with her ticket clipper as she strode out.

Enginemen could find themselves on a variety of duties, and George checked the schedule to discover that he and Danny were to take a local pick-up goods for a week. This duty was not completely onerous but it could be boring. It meant taking a few vehicles, vans or wagons, along a route, stopping at all stations to pick up and drop off goods at all of them. It usually required some shunting in the one or two sidings that each small station had and, if need be, dealing with occasional cattle for market. Parcels could be placed in the guard's van but larger items such as bulk feed for animals or seed bags for local farmers went into the wagons, lifted if necessary by means of a small hand-operated crane in the yard. Some station yards also had a cattle pen – a short, fenced and gated platform where cattle or sheep could be held until loaded. When staff were notified, the next available pick-up train would contain a cattle wagon. The cattle wagon had separate compartments in which cattle could be securely packed, to avoid injury when the train was on the move.

On one of his first pick-up runs, George had an old 0-6-0T pannier tank with Danny as his fireman. Danny was known at the shed for his practical jokes. He had already tried to tease George but had discovered that his tricks backfired badly if his driver was the victim.

Danny's knowledge of the countryside was wide and informative; he and his brother had been brought up on a farm, which his brother David still ran, raising cattle and pigs with a few sheep for good measure. George enjoyed listening to Danny's tales of life in the country but had never realised exactly how hard it could be. The two boys had to walk three miles every day to school and then back home again, regardless of the weather, which could easily be two feet of snow in winter.

Once on the morning pick-up goods, they pulled in at a small station and backed their short train into a cattle siding. George saw a few cattle waiting in the pens, ready to be loaded.

"The bull is for the local show and the three cows are for the market in Bristol," said the station porter as he opened the doors of the cattle wagon.

"Whose are the cows?" asked Danny curiously, "They look like some David had."

"Aye, that they are," said the porter, "he's had some bad luck, and – oh, here he is."

David Butler didn't look happy as he came up to his brother. "Hello Danny, I have to sell these three."

"What's up, David? Why're you selling the cows?"

"It's that rich sod Simmonds, next door; he wants to buy my land but I won't sell. So he's gone and dammed part of the stream on his land, and the little that flows through to mine isn't enough water for all my cattle."

"Sorry to hear that, David." Danny eyed the bull in the neighbouring pen, "That his prize bull?"

David looked at it. "Yes, that's his."

"We'll have to get moving, Danny," said George, interrupting their chat, "so let the porter load the cattle otherwise we'll be running late."

"Right, cheerio, David, we'll look after your cows for you."

The bull was loaded first and Danny jumped into the cattle wagon to pin the partition and help the loading of his brother's cows into the remaining space of the van.

At the next little station, Danny said, "I'll just look into the cattle wagon and check that all's in order."

George frowned, "Why wouldn't it be?"

"You never know with cattle."

"Fine then," George was town-bred and knew next to nothing about farming; he always believed in allowing work to be done by people who were experts at it.

Danny climbed back into the cab. "All ship-shape and Bristol fashion."

Yet all did not appear to be well; the cattle wagon seemed to be shaking somewhat.

They offloaded the bull later in the morning, to be taken to the local cattle show, while the remaining cattle stayed in the wagon to be taken back to Bristol for sale, but Danny came back with an anxious appearance on his face.

"Bit of a problem with the cows," he said to George, "can't sell them in their condition. I noticed something David missed. We'll drop them back off for him to pick up on the return trip."

"If you're sure."

"Oh, I'm quite sure."

George shook his head, assuming Danny knew what he was about.

"You'd better let your brother know we're bringing his cows back."

"Yeah, I'll ring through to the station and get someone to pop over and tell him."

David was waiting as they pulled into the station yard once more. His unhappiness was plain on his face; "What did I miss about the cows?" he demanded.

Danny went over to him and spoke to him quietly. The frown on David's face turned to a slow grin and he began to chuckle.

"Your brother didn't seem unduly worried about the problem with his cows," commented George as they pulled away once more, "What was the problem with them?"

"They're actually too valuable to sell," replied Danny, "they're all pregnant! They must first produce calves before he can sell them."

"Pregnant? They didn't look pregnant to me as they were put in; mind you, I'm no expert."

"No," smiled Danny, "when they went into the wagon, they weren't pregnant; but-" he grinned, "they are now!"

"But how-?" Slow understanding spread over George's face. "The wagon's shaking! You can't have fastened the partition properly and the bull got at the cows and serviced them!" He leaned back, and laughed in delight. "But what about your brother's water shortage? He won't be able to give them enough water."

"No problem there, George. I've had a quiet word with Ben the porter here; he helps all the firemen when their engines need topping up!"

"You've got it all sewn up, haven't you?"

"Blood's thicker than water," commented Danny, "that's one in the eye for Jack Simmonds. Those heifers will bear prize calves and fetch our David good money; and all because Simmonds is too lousy to fork out for a separate cattle wagon for his prize bull! Serve the bastard right."

16 - George gets an inside opinion (November 1927)

Like a good many GWR staff, George was feeling very smug at the reception the Americans had given to their visitor, the brand new *King George V* express passenger locomotive at the celebrations organised by the Baltimore and Ohio Railroad. The British 4-6-0, with its clean lines and power in such a small size (compared to most American locomotives), and its smooth running, had deeply impressed them. Some of the later United States engines had even appeared with a copper cap to their chimneys!

However, sitting in a Swindon pub one evening, George met a staff member who did not share his enthusiasm; Geoffrey Fairbrother was drowning his sorrows in his beer when George joined him at a table because he noticed a small GWR staff badge on the man's lapel.

"You don't look too happy," commented George as he sat down with his own glass. "Aren't you proud of what the GWR has achieved? The strongest express passenger engine in Britain winning plaudits in the United States and even here with some of the best locomotives in the country?"

What George was claiming was hardly open to doubt. Under Collett - the Chief Mechanical Engineer - the GWR had continued to build along the lines laid down 30 years earlier by Mr Churchward, who had developed the GWR locomotive fleet with engines whose basic design was to last until the end of steam.

"No, I won't deny that," replied Geoffrey. "What I object to is the

LMS wasting its time in these past four years."

"I don't understand," said George, "what's your concern with the LMS?"

"I'm an ex-LNWR man," said Geoffrey. "I began work in the drawing office in Crewe in 1909 and we had some fine engines. Our Claughtons had some design problems but the war came to stop progress and then after it ended, the CME, Bowen-Cook, died before he could deal with the problems. We thought the L&Y man, Hughes, would sort it, but he retired." He went on to explain at some length how LMS motive power engineering was then dominated by "Midland men" from Derby, who were "useless". According to Geoffrey Fairbrother, their only decent engines were the 4-4-0 Compounds and the 4Fs, but the Compounds couldn't handle the Scottish expresses without double-heading. The 4Fs, Geoffrey considered satisfactory freight engines, but they suffered constantly with overheating bearings.

George took a breath, and tried to offer an opinion but Geoffrey was on a roll. "They didn't put any serious effort into the LNWR's big express passenger Claughtons, apart from putting bigger boilers in them – to supply more steam to offset leaky valves; there was bugger all attempt to correct the minor faults. They haven't bothered to do anything with any of the LNWR engines, or the L&Y's locomotives. They just keep on building to their own poor designs."

"But I thought the LMS had some powerful Beyer-Garretts for their heavy freight work?" George finally got a word in.

"Oh yes, but the silly buggers tried to tell Beyer-Garrett how to design them, as if they didn't know! And they insisted on putting Midland features into the engines. The result? Engines which spend far too much time in the repair shops, and they are widely regarded as failures."

"They should have looked at our 28 class 2-8-0s! They're fine goods engines."

Geoffrey stared at George. "D'you know why I left the LMS?"

"No - why?"

"They asked Swindon to build them some of their Castles, and when Swindon replied that they were too busy, they asked for drawings of the engines but were refused, so, under Mr Henry Fowler's superintendency, they went to the Southern and got drawings for their new Lord Nelson class express passenger locomotives, got outside companies to build them, and then bestowed grand names on them, the Royal Scots. I thought, if the new LMS can't design and build decent engines themselves, I'm off to a company which can."

"So you came to the Great Western?"

"Of course - look what your Mr Collett has done; he's improved the Stars to produce the Castle class and, as if that wasn't enough, he's had your great King class designed, built, and even modified - all within nine months! No wonder the Yanks love it!"

"So what do the LMS put on their Scottish expresses these days?"

"They still use the Claughtons and the big L&Y Dreadnoughts, although I have to say the new Royal Scots seem to be able to cope single-handed with all but the heaviest trains. Perhaps they've finally got something right!"

When George returned home one evening, Alice greeted him with a serious expression.

"What's up, love?" he enquired.

"It's a letter from Taunton, George. Your dad's very ill, and his neighbour advises you to go and see him."

George went cold. He and Alice had made a point of visiting Henry in Taunton every few weeks, so he had known his father was off colour for some time. The old man had never got over the loss of his wife. Although he had struggled on working for another five years after her death, he had lost the passion for the job that had stood him in such good stead. He had been made Driver at the remarkably early age of 33 and had loved his job, although he always maintained that his favourite driving had been particularly in his years on the old broad gauge. After his retirement, he had intended to buy a small cottage near the sea and potter around in a small boat, but had never got round to the effort of finding somewhere.

George and Alice planned to spend a couple of days in Taunton to see what could be done for Henry. They found there was very little; Henry was already bedridden and managed only with the help of the neighbour who had contacted George. She was spending more time with Henry than with her own elderly husband, who didn't mind. He and Henry had known each other for many years and he understood that his good friend only had days left. In the event, Henry Denton passed away peacefully in his sleep the day after George and Alice arrived.

Alice was worried for her husband for some days after his father's death; he had never talked a lot about Henry, but she knew there had been a deep, if unvoiced, love between them. George was unusually quiet after the funeral and didn't even pay as much attention to their son Ben as he would normally. But an unexpected change in his work shift seemed to bring him out of his melancholy.

He was called to assist on a 'foreign' railway - as non-GWR railways were known. The Somerset & Dorset Joint Railway was short of a driver and the GWR was asked if it could assist as neither the Southern Railway nor the London, Midland and Scottish - jointly responsible for the line - had spare enginemen. Although he had been along it once or twice with a GWR freight from Bristol to Wells, George did not know the Bath to Bournemouth road well and was therefore required to learn it, and to get used to the mainly LMS locomotives which, along with the coaching stock, were still painted in the Prussian Blue of the S&DJR. He found it strange to be driving the Midland Railway-built 4-4-0s and wondered why they had supplied such underpowered locomotives for what was a fairly difficult route over the Mendip Hills. But then, the Midland Railway had rarely built anything of real power, except for a few heavy freight 2-8-0s especially for the S&DJR and the remarkable 0-10-0 engine, referred to as the Lickey banker, for banking trains over the steep incline at Lickey on the Midland main line from Bristol to Birmingham.

George had spent his first day observing in the cab of the S&D 4-4-0, looking out for the signals and generally learning the road, before taking over as a temporary driver the following week.

He had joined the regular crew at Bath and was now in the local passenger to Bournemouth; he would return later in the day. He noticed how the regular crew had to work their locomotive hard over the hilly run and realised that this was not going to be an easy duty. They had a number of through carriages from Newcastle and Manchester to Bournemouth, with a range of designs here from the teak of the LNER and the red of the LMS making an interesting splash of colour in contrast with the blue of the rest of the train. This duty entailed double-heading such an important through train and was a task beyond the capability of a single 4-4-0.

George's month-long stint on the S&D gave him one bad moment, when he was approaching Evercreech Junction with another heavy long-distance train; he had begun to slow well before it was technically required and his fireman was staring at him in surprise. "What are you-?" he began, when the emergency brake went on. Someone had pulled the emergency cord that ran right through the train. It was brought to a standstill about 100 yards short of the platform and George looked out along the length of it to see a wisp of smoke pouring from underneath one of the coaches.

"I think we've got a hot box," he said to the fireman, "go and have a quick shufti."

The fireman returned quickly. "Yep, that's what it is, but the punters are getting upset."

"We'll just pull slowly into the station and then we can get them all out and into another coach. They can put that one off and fix the problem in Highbridge."

A hot box was when one of the axleboxes, filled with grease or oil, overheated and began to burn. The normal procedure was to stop, detach the offending vehicle, and continue the journey, leaving the local fitters to fix the problem. There was no spare coach readily available as a substitute for the faulty vehicle, so the disturbed passengers were most unhappy at being turned out of their seats, especially as the rest of the train was fairly full. The guard, however, was unsympathetic: "Well, you can stay here if you like, but this coach will be taken off the train and shunted into a siding for attention. Should only take a day or two."

"Your railway shouldn't have such dangerous coaches! No wonder you're called the Slow and Dirty!" complained one elderly lady on the platform to the guard. He pointed at the coach's dark red colour and said simply, "Not one of ours, madam, it's an LMS coach. Ours are blue." And he stalked off before she could think of a sufficiently biting riposte.

In the cab as they moved off again after a short delay, the fireman looked at George and said, "You were very quick in putting the brake on, Mr Denton."

"Of course; you can't run a passenger train if you've got a hot box," commented George shortly.

"But you began to slow us down before you knew we had a hot box," said the fireman.

"Nonsense," replied George. The fireman just shook his head and didn't reply, but he was puzzled; he knew that George had begun to slow the train before the emergency brake had gone on. How had he known there was a problem?

He would have been even more puzzled if he had known what George himself was thinking. *He's right. Why on earth did I begin to slow the train down when I did?*

17 - Three eventful trips (April 1933)

George had by now been driving for several years and had been transferred to Bristol's Bath Road shed from St Philip's Marsh. Bath Road dealt with passenger traffic and George was already regarded as one of its best drivers. Furthermore, he was expected to be promoted into the top link before much longer, running the expresses to Paddington, Plymouth, and South Wales. The semi-fasts to Swindon and the West Country were already his bread and butter, and his timekeeping was widely accepted as being exemplary. This gave rise to occasional jealousy among the rather more lax drivers, but even they had to admit that he could get more effort out of a steam locomotive than many of his older colleagues. He was also known for giving his more competent firemen a chance at the regulator from time to time. On one occasion, however, this habit was to backfire very badly.

They had taken over a Plymouth to Paddington semi-fast at Newton Abbot and were running down Wellington bank near Taunton; Fireman Jerry Hampton was on the regulator while George took a hand on the shovel. As they passed a small copse, George happened to glance out of the cab of their Hall class 4-6-0 and saw a man race out of the copse and head straight for the tracks. The man was fewer than 100 yards away but had clearly not seen the train. George sounded the whistle frantically but the man was looking over his shoulder at three policemen who were running after him. George leaned over and grabbed the regulator out of the startled fireman's hand and yanked it down.

"Brake!" he yelled at Jerry, but it was far too late; the man was stumbling over the track when the locomotive buffers hit him.

George was able to pull up several hundred yards further along and he ordered Jerry to put the vacuum brake firmly on while he rushed back to see the police, who were by this time gathered round the mangled body.

The constable who saw George approaching directed him to the sergeant, who had his notebook out and was writing busily in it. George caught a brief glimpse of the corpse before the sergeant began to question him and note down his responses.

"What speed were you doing, Driver, when you hit the man?"

George shook his head. "I don't know, Sergeant; most of our locomotives don't have speedometers, but I would guess we were doing about 40 miles per hour; we were beginning to accelerate down the bank."

"Well, I don't suppose it matters anyway, there would have been nothing you could have done. Anyone who runs across a railway track without looking for trains is asking for trouble. Would your fireman agree with what you just said?"

"Actually, I was firing at the time; I had just given my mate a break so he was on the regulator on the right-hand side of the cab and wouldn't have seen anything, but you can ask him. I'll send him over."

George returned to the cab and sent Jerry to be questioned. The fireman returned ten minutes later, looking extremely pale.

"I j-just killed a man, George!" he stuttered. He was evidently very badly shaken.

George tried to calm him. "No you didn't, Jerry, the man killed himself. You could never have stopped the train in time. No blame can be attached to you at all."

"But, but-"

"Now Jerry, stop and think: what weight is our whole train with its nine corridors?"

"Errm... close to 400 tonnes."

"Correct, and we were doing about 40 downhill. How long before we could stop in an emergency?"

"I dunno – 500 yards?"

"Something like that. So even if you had seen him, which you couldn't have, being on the right in the cab, what could you have done?"

"I could have slowed the train!"

"Indeed you could have. We'd have hit him at 36 miles an hour instead of 40. What difference would that have made?"

"Well, if you put it like that-"

"How else could you put it?"

For the rest of the shift, Jerry was shaking like a leaf and found it hard to concentrate on his work. The next day, he was nowhere to be seen and the shed foreman announced that Fireman Hampton had left the Great Western Railway. His colleagues all understood – it was hard to know that you had been instrumental in killing someone, even when you knew it was not your fault; it was a well-known but rarely mentioned hazard of the job.

George tried hard to forget the episode and he turned his attention to his son Ben, now six years old; they were busy with their latest project. George had built a garden shed and he and Ben were constructing a model railway for the garden. George had bought parts to lay the track and Ben was shown how to lay the sleepers and tack the tiny chairs in place to hold the rails in position. They already had two engines and three coaches, plus a few wagons. Running the railway with his dad on the weekend was Ben's greatest delight and the grin on his face helped to take George's mind off the recent tragic shift.

A few months after his disastrous trip from Plymouth, on checking the schedule, George discovered that he was booked on a Bristol to Paddington express for the first time. He had already been to London on freights and semi-fasts several times and had formally learned the road. This was a heavy express with its added timetable demands. The locomotive was a King class 4-6-0, the most powerful express passenger locomotive the Great Western had, and a class which George had not driven before. There was no particular difficulty about this, as GWR locomotives tended to be standardised and a King was very similar to the highly successful Castle class 4-6-0, which he had frequently driven. George had heard from one or two drivers that in fact the Kings, in spite of their statistics, were no better than Castles, but as he pulled away with the fourteen coaches, he began to form an entirely different opinion. Certainly fourteen on would have been no problem at all for a Castle, yet even so this King seemed to George to have the edge on anything he had previously driven. Admittedly, it was one of the 1930 batch and therefore only three years old, but both the power and smooth acceleration were, he felt, superior to that of the Castles.

The run from Temple Meads as far as Swindon was broadly uphill; in designing the route 100 years previously, I.K. Brunel had chosen

Swindon as the midpoint for engine changing, but now engines were usually only changed there if they needed to go into the works for attention. The run from Swindon to Paddington was for George a truly exhilarating experience; the signalmen were obviously primed to let the express through and he was therefore hardly held at a signal at all. He was still doing over 70 through Old Oak Common. As he drew up at the buffer stops in Paddington he only had one regret; his father had retired just before the Kings had been built and so had never had the chance to drive one. He would have enjoyed it immensely, thought George.

George's next shift included a semi-fast from Plymouth to Manchester and Liverpool via Hereford and Shrewsbury, but he was disappointed to see that instead of the Hall he had expected, one of the few remaining County class 4-4-0s had been readied in the shed for him. Like most of his colleagues, he did not like these engines; they were handy for the shorter distance runs and were fast and powerful, but they were very unsteady and the cab ride in them was no picnic, especially as they got older. The rumour was that they had been built because the LNWR, which owned the Hereford-Salop line jointly with the GWR, did not like big 4-6-0s along the route, although later their own big Claughton 4-6-0s were found on it from time to time.

Nevertheless, the County took the nine-coach train away with ease and it handled the first part of the run to Hereford with no more than the expected swaying and rolling. However, once past Hereford, the run became rapidly more unpleasant; clearly, this engine was nearing the end of its days. Fireman Fred Compton was having great difficulty getting the coal into the fire as the shaking and rattling was making it almost impossible to throw it into the firebox with any degree of accuracy, and the fire – and consequently the steaming - was suffering as a result. George was strongly tempted to fail his engine at Church Stretton, but the knowledge that a replacement locomotive would not be available before Shrewsbury persuaded him to persevere.

The train was due to change engines at Shrewsbury and on bringing his engine to the GWR shed at Coleham, George reported that he believed the engine was unfit for further service.

"I am sorry, Driver," said the shedmaster on hearing this, "we have no possible replacement engine and she's booked for the return to Bristol; what's more," he added, "you're booked to take her back. But I'll at least get a fitter to look her over and we'll do what we can."

"No chance, I suppose," said George nodding to the LMS shed next door, "of getting a North-Western engine as a replacement?"

The shedmaster laughed. "No, not the slightest chance; we've already borrowed two of theirs this week and our accountants are complaining bitterly at the cost."

"Then they may be complaining again soon if I have to fail her on the way back," grumbled George. "You'd better warn Hereford to have something ready. I can't see us getting back to Bristol unless your fitters can do something drastic."

"We'll do our best."

But whatever the fitters had been able to achieve had little effect; on the return run, the engine was almost as rough as it had been on the outward journey.

"Crikey, I'm sorry George!" shouted Fred as his shovelful missed the firebox entirely and strewed coal all over the cab floor yet again.

"Not your fault, Fred," called George, "it won't go into my journal. I'm going to have to fail her in Hereford. You can pop out at Leominster and warn them to let Hereford know we'll need to change engines there. They won't like it."

Nor did they. The Hereford shedmaster was waiting on the platform as they drew in 30 minutes late.

"Now, Driver, what's the problem with this engine?"

"She is so rough, sir, we can't fire her. We had a passenger come up to the cab in Church Stretton to enquire whether we would be staying on the rails all the way. There were further complaints at Leominster, and it's impossible to keep her steady at any speed as she's rolling and knocking so much."

"Well I'm sorry, Driver Denton, but you'll have to take her through to Temple Meads. I've been on the phone to your boss and he tells me that if anyone can drive her, you can."

They struggled with a very poor steaming engine and barely managed to reach Bristol; their arrival was an hour and ten minutes late, and George was only slightly mollified by the shedmaster's next words: "Don't worry, George; she's off to the Swindon scrapyard on Tuesday and she is our last County, so you won't be driving one again."

George returned home that evening with a smile on his face.

"Why the smile?" asked Alice curiously.

"I think I've driven a County class engine for the last time," said

George. "They're strong and fast but my goodness they can be very rough in the cab. The newer Halls are much better."

"What makes you think you've driven a County for the last time?" asked Alice.

"They're all being scrapped, thankfully," replied her husband, "the last ones are going to the Swindon scrapyard.'

Some weeks later on George's birthday, Ben came into the kitchen, grinning; "Daddy, didn't you say you've driven a County for the last time?"

"Yes, I did, why?"

"I think you are mistaken," said the lad, "come with me." Ben took his father by the hand and led him into the garden shed. There on the model railway was a birthday card leaning up against a brand new model engine with a 4-4-0 wheel arrangement.

It was Hornby's *County of Bedford*.

18 – George meets a young cleaner (January 1936)

After several years of marriage, George and Alice still had fond memories of their honeymoon in the North West. When a vacancy occurred for a driver in Chester, George asked Alice whether she would like to move there. She said yes without hesitation so George applied for, and was granted, the transfer. Having already served a stint in Wellington, his route knowledge of the area was extensive, and Sidney Thomson, the shed foreman there, welcomed the addition to his team of a driver with a growing reputation. One day shortly after his arrival, George had taken a train of empty coal wagons to Cardiff and was returning with a mixed freight from Abergavenny to Shrewsbury when he was held up at a signal near a siding not far south of Hereford. The siding had been clearly unused for some time as its rails were rusty.

"Time for a brew, d'you think?" asked Mervyn Jones, George's fireman.

"We could try."

"I'll fill the can and-" Mervyn's face turned pale; "oh bugger, I've got the runs! I'll nip out in to the field quickly!" He climbed down hurriedly and disappeared into the nearby bushes.

While Mervyn was otherwise engaged, George watched a short down freight consisting of only half a dozen vans drawn by a Pannier tank engine pull into the siding and disappear round a curve. George frowned. He didn't recognise the guard, he was sure he had glimpsed an army officer inside the guard compartment, and three of the vans were shocvans. Furthermore, all of them were completely nondescript; there was no indication as to who they belonged to or what they contained. As soon as the train had gone, a soldier in camouflage dress with a can and what seemed to be a paint brush appeared from behind a bush; he scrutinised George's train but didn't notice George. He bent down and began to paint the rail surfaces a rusty brown. When he had finished, he slipped quickly out of sight again.

Hmm, thought George, *something the Army doesn't want anyone to know about. Must be a secret base.* He was to hear a little more about this base five years later.

After a few minutes, Mervyn climbed into the cab once more.

"All in order?" queried George.

"God, I hope so," muttered Mervyn, "but I've got a bloody painful arse."

"See anything unusual, while you were in the bushes?"

"Nope; should I have?"

"Just wondered. Er - why the painful bottom?"

"I didn't have any paper, and I grabbed some leaves to clean myself."

"So?"

"They were nettles"

"Oof!" winced George, "We'll see if we can get some salve in Hereford crews' cabin."

"Oh yes please!"

The following day, George and Mervyn were returning from their

Wolverhampton run and Mervyn had finally ceased complaining about his rear-end difficulties, although he was still reluctant to sit down in the station breaks. He climbed down from the cab and uncoupled their Castle from its train. A small Pannier 0-6-0 attached itself to the last three coaches, drew them out, and shunted them into a carriage siding for cleaning, to remain in Chester where they would be reattached to a Paddington express later in the day. A 41 class 2-6-2T coupled up to the remaining seven and, having received the guard's flag, moved off with them on the final leg of the journey to Birkenhead Woodside. Once the line was clear, George backed the Castle class 4-6-0 out to the end of the platform, waited for the starter signal, and when it showed 'clear' backed the big engine out, over the station throat, and into the shed for servicing.

The shed foreman came out and called George over to his office.

"George, I would like you to do me a favour," he began, "I have a promising new lad; I'd like your opinion on him. He's just joined us from Saltney and is a Passed Cleaner. He's a bit rough round the edges and needs polishing, but I have a feeling that he may be useful. Could you take him for a week and then let me know what you think?"

"Of course I will, Sid," replied George. "What's his name and when do I get him?"

"His name's Lance Hargreaves, and you'll have him next week. Oh, and I want you to take a light engine, a Star class 4-6-0, to Swindon; they want it in a hurry for something – they didn't say what. It's in good nick, so it can't be for repairs. You'll need to leave tomorrow at 4.50am."

Geoffrey Fairbrother was sitting in his favourite Swindon pub, moodily sipping his ale, when George walked in. George paused, stared at Geoffrey, frowning and wondering where he had seen the man before. He smiled as he realised it had been in this same pub some years previously. He ordered his pint and then and walked over to him.

"I've met you before, sitting here a fair while back," he said, sitting down at the same table. "You didn't look happy then, and don't look too happy now; what's the problem this time?"

Geoffrey looked up at him, frowning, then his face cleared. "Oh yes, Driver Denton, isn't it?"

"I'm based up north now, in Chester; just down for a double home turn; I can only allow myself one pint - back this evening on a Saltney freight via Gloucester."

"Congratulations," said Geoffrey, absentmindedly. "No, I'm wondering whether I made the right move when I left the LMS eleven years ago."

"Ah yes, I remember now – you were complaining about the Midland men running the motive power design, weren't you?"

"Yes, I thought I was in a backward-looking company, but I sometimes think I'm in a backward-looking company again."

George was surprised to hear this from a now presumably fairly senior draftsman in the Swindon drawing office. "Why do you say that?"

"I caught a glimpse of a letter last week; it must have slipped out of a bag of old correspondence due for burning. It was sent two years ago from Mr Stanier to Mr Collett, his old boss."

William Stanier had been appointed Chief Mechanical Engineer to the LMS; he had been Collett's assistant at Swindon but the two men were the same age so Stanier could not expect to take over when his boss retired. Under Stanier's strong direction, the LMS were now producing excellent locomotives.

"And-?"

"You probably realise that Stanier's Princess class Pacifics are basically his version of our Kings, which he worked on. Well, he'd found a solution to one of the little problems our Kings have, and sent the idea to Collett so that he could fix them, but it was ignored and the Kings still have the problem. We hear he's now building something even better; bigger 4-6-2s that will eclipse Gresley's Pacifics on the LNER."

"Yes, I've heard quite a lot about Stanier's engines; his class five general purpose engines are based on our Halls, which he also worked on when he was with us and they are already getting quite a reputation."

"He's putting the LMS ahead of us!"

"He's building good engines, I'll give you that, but then he would, wouldn't he – he's an ex-GWR man – we trained him."

"But we're getting behind! I didn't want to work for a company that's complacent!" grumbled Geoffrey. "It's such a pity we've lost Mr Churchward, he would've listened." The Great Western's previous Chief Mechanical Engineer, G.J. Churchward, had died three years earlier in an accident.

George took a pull at his pint. "Right," he said, as he placed his glass carefully back on the beer mat, "now; what is the purpose of a railway company?"

Geoffrey looked up in surprise, "To provide a satisfactory transport service to the public."

"Right, and don't we do that?"

"Suppose."

"And what can his Princess Pacifics do that our Kings can't?"

Geoffrey smiled at that; "They can run for six hours non-stop with sixteen on."

"And what six-hour, non-stop run have we got on the Great Western?"

Geoffrey thought for a moment. "Hmm! Paddington to Plymouth is only four hours. And the Kings aren't allowed over Saltash Bridge, of course."

"Stanier's Pacifics wouldn't be, either. The Kings don't go north of Wolverhampton; the traffic doesn't warrant it. But that's not all. Our Kings are masters of all the really heavy passenger work we have. We don't need any more. And if we did, we'd build more of them. We have enough Castles and Stars for the other heavy expresses, and we have sufficient Halls and Saints for the rest of the passenger trains."

"What about freights? The 28 class 2-8-0s were basically designed in 1903!"

"So? Our 28s manage the freights very well and for the few express freights, we've got the bigger 47s. No, friend, we already have the tools we need for our jobs; although we hear there are new designs being prepared to replace some of our older Moguls, but I imagine you would know more about that than me."

Geoffrey nodded. "Perhaps you're right; and yes, there are a couple of new designs on the way. There's another 4-6-0 with smaller wheels for the heavier general work and a light 4-6-0 to replace the older Moguls, which are getting life-expired."

"Well there you are, then; we're not really getting behind at all! It's all a question of meeting quite different business needs."

A day or so later, George was enjoying a tea break in the Chester enginemen's cabin when he overheard a conversation between a young man he didn't know and a fireman.

"You got on alright with her, then?"

The young man shrugged, "She was fine – but a bit skinny fer me."

"Thin? But will you be going out with her again?"

"Nah; I reckon she's got two thimbles on a bit o' string fer a brassiere."

The fireman laughed. "Lance, you're hopeless!"

"Why, wot's wrong with that?"

"Never mind."

George walked over to the young man. "You're Lance Hargreaves?"

"Yep."

"I'm George Denton. You'll be driving with me next week."

"Oh yeah, Mr Thomson already told me. Pleased ter meet yer, Mr Denton."

George nodded. *At least the lad's got some manners,* he thought to himself. "I'll see you next week then."

"Yeah, ta!"

Their first duty together was a pick-up goods with a 2-6-0 *Mogul* as far as Corwen in North Wales. George watched young Lance surreptitiously, as the latter climbed into the cab. He checked the gauges and peeped into the fire, throwing a couple of shovelfuls exactly where they were needed. George watched with approval. Lance brushed the few scraps of coal dust from the cab floor and finally he looked out to see whether the signal was clear for them to start; it wasn't, but instead of sitting down to wait, he checked the fire again.

Promising, thought George. "Which roads do you know already, young Lance?" he asked.

"I've bin up to Salop a couple a times, down to Birken'ead, an' let's think; along ter Llangollen a few times, an' o' course shunted in Saltney as well as 'ere several times, Mr Denton."

"You've already got some useful road knowledge, then."

"Yeah, I s'pose so."

"And you've fired on all these routes?"

"Well, most of 'em."

But George noticed that in spite of the questioning, the lad still checked to see whether the starter showed clear for them to move off while he was answering George's questions.

The run as far as Wrexham could be a testing one if the locomotive was due for some attention, as this Mogul was. It was one of the original batch built in 1913 and had seen better days, yet Lance Hargreaves had no difficulty in handling the fire and keeping steam up over the steep Gresford Bank, although he was glad of the chance to stop in the yard there and shunt, detaching and coupling up a few vans and wagons as required. There were pauses for picking up and dropping off vehicles at both Ruabon and Llangollen, and George had been entertained by the comments of the young man regarding his amorous adventures. During his service in the Great War, George himself had been no slouch regarding experiences with Parisian ladies of dubious virtue, but he had to admit that young Passed Cleaner Hargreaves was in a much higher league than he had been. Nevertheless, in spite of his chatter, Lance's mind never left his firing; he constantly checked the gauges and the fire, and he gave timely warning to George regarding all the signals which he was familiar with. At Corwen, they handed the train over to an Aberystwyth crew while they had a 90-minute break, before returning with a semi-fast passenger to Birkenhead.

At the end of the trial week, George was able to tell Sid Thomson that they had acquired a very promising young engineman whom George would be very pleased to have as his regular fireman.

"He is a lecherous young lad, Sid, by the sound of things, but he knows his stuff well."

"Yes, George, his reputation in Saltney as quite a lad for 'tom-catting around' has obviously been well-deserved," remarked Sid, "but that has little bearing on his work, as far as I can see."

Neither George nor Sid were to know that Chester Shed was about to acquire a team which would in the next fifteen years become one of the finest crews in the whole of the Wolverhampton Division.

19 – Lance oversteps the mark (April 1937)

"George, I want you and young Hargreaves to take a local passenger to Wellington and from there you'll be taking another local to Crewe; Hargreaves can come back on the cushions. I understand you already know the road from your earlier duties at Wellington?" Sid Thomson was in his office, explaining an unusual shift roster.

"Yes, that's right, Sid, although the signalling may have changed since then."

"No it hasn't; I checked. And it's only for a couple of days; Wellington's a man short."

"Shouldn't be a problem, then."

They had an elderly but free-running Bulldog 4-4-0 to Wellington with six corridors, which the locomotive managed with ease. In the station, the platform inspector told Lance to return to Salop in the cab of a light engine, which was returning to its home shed where it was to await a return shift to Chester. George walked to his new duty surprised to see the Crewe train ready with unusual motive power; a 'Dukedog' 4-4-0 - so-called by enginemen because it was an amalgam of old but proven engines, namely Bulldog frames and works with a Duke class boiler and cab. These clever reconstructions were only two years old but naturally looked very old-fashioned. They had initially been given the names of Earls but the revered gentlemen had strongly objected to having their names on such small and ancient-looking engines, so the GWR removed the names and put them on their new and modern Castle class 4-6-0s. Nevertheless, these quaint engines were versatile and very suited to light passenger work on the ex-Cambrian Railway lines, and they were popular with enginemen. They were also very popular with GWR head office as they were technically rebuilt engines and therefore did not add to the company's capital stock; something the bean counters would have frowned upon.

George was pleased as he had never driven one before and was eager to see what they were like to drive. Dickie Wentworth, the Wellington fireman, simply nodded. "Nowt wrong wi' 'em," he said. Dickie was a man of few words.

George wondered what it was about Wellington that seemed to encourage taciturn firemen; he was put in mind of Josh Simpson, who had also had little to say.

The run to Crewe seemed to back up Dickie's words; the Dukedog took the six coaches with ease and pulled into a south bay platform in Crewe right on time. A few minutes after all the passengers had left the train, a small LMS tank engine drew the coaches away and George and Dickie waited for the platform starter signal to let them out and away to Crewe's small GWR shed at Gresty Lane. While they were waiting, one of Mr Stanier's 2-6-4T tank engines pulled in on the adjacent line with a local train from Stoke. Its driver looked out of his cab at them and called over to them, "Where in hell did you dig that old crate from?"

Dickie leaned out of the cab. "It's the oldest we could find. Crewe don't deserve owt better!" he cackled. The LMS engineman's grinning reply was unprintable.

Their return to Wellington was similar to the outward run; Dickie fired carefully and with skill but without saying very much. Oddly enough, the following day produced another derisive comment from a nearby LMS engineman which, in its turn, induced Dickie to react in similar fashion, much to George's amusement.

George's next run was another unusual one; he and Lance were to take the local passenger service to West Kirby via Hooton, where they had to reverse the train. Here they would uncouple the engine and return past their train to couple up once more to the rear, then they would travel bunker-first along the West Wirral line through Neston and Parkgate to West Kirby before returning the same way. For this duty they used one of the large Prairie 2-6-2Ts, which had no trouble managing the six non-corridors. These big, powerful engines were designed for the London and Birmingham commuter services and could handle almost twice the load if required. With their enclosed cabs, they were unpleasant on hot summer days but conversely very welcome in the cold winters.

At Chester shed, George was pleased to note that Lance was already in the cab: seeing to the fire, checking the injectors, and ensuring that the steam pressure was already rising, to enable them to get away to the station to pick up their train. When he took the can to oil the outside motion, however, he found that there was already enough on the bearings. He climbed under the engine to oil the big ends; this clearly hadn't been done. This puzzled him as the engine had been standing all night and the fire raisers didn't have access to the oil; it had to be fetched by the individual engine crew each day from the supply stores and was carefully checked out. He climbed back into the cab.

"Lance, did you collect the oil this morning?"

"Yes, Mr Denton, first thing."

"Well, where is it?"

"Er – I were a bit early so after I checked the fire and steam pressure and cleaned up the cab, I oiled the motion. I seen you do it lotsa times an' it seemed easy, like, so I thought I'd save yer a bit of-"

"You *oiled the motion*?" George could not believe his ears.

"Yeah, is there summat wrong?"

"You're damn right there is!" George's anger showed in his face. Lance blanched; he had never seen his driver upset before, nor heard him use strong language. "You're not even a fireman! Passed cleaners or firemen do not oil the motion; that is a job for the driver. He knows what he's doing and he does it because he is the one who gets the blame if an engine seizes up on his shift. Did you oil the big ends?"

"Err-"

"What about the cylinders?"

"Umm-"

"If I hadn't checked, we'd have seized up somewhere near Mollington! We'd never even have reached Capenhurst."

"I'm really sorry, Mr D-"

"Never mind being sorry, my lad. Stick to your own duties and *never, ever* try and do my job again. I like my job and I want to keep it; I don't want some young sprog still wet behind the ears ruining my engine!"

Lance nodded miserably; he had enjoyed working with George and felt that he was getting somewhere. Now he had badly blotted his copybook and could conceivably face the sack.

For the remainder of their shift, their total conversation was limited to the bare minimum required while George calmed down. Lance would have been very relieved to know that George never had any intention of taking action about the incident because he saw that in spite of his youth, Lance had all the makings of a good engineman. In any case, in his army days George had learned how an apparent loss of temper – something most good teachers knew to use on rare occasions - could firmly impart an important message to young learners.

During the next few days, the atmosphere in the cab began very gradually to relax as George reduced the level of anxiety on the part of his mate, but it was to be another fortnight before they were both back to their previous level of ease with one another.

A few months later, George was back in the shedmaster's office.

"George, I have a problem you might be able to help me with."

"What is it?"

"Freddy Birchwood has just been taken ill, so I need a replacement crew for the 7.30 from Wrexham for at least a week."

"The auto train?"

"Yes, d'you think that your young Hargreaves can be trusted on his own in a cab?"

George thought then said, "Yes. I had to bounce him a while back when he stepped out of line, but I straightened him out. I'm sure I could trust him now."

In an auto train, the engine was not always at the front; it might be between two coaches or at the rear. The driver was in a special cab in the front coach and signalled his orders to the fireman by means of a cord along the train. The system normally worked well with a crew who knew what they were doing.

George was certain that he and Lance could manage between them, and it would show Lance that his driver had faith in him once more; a fine method of cementing a good team together. The big advantage of these autotrains, common on smaller branch lines in the Great Western, was that there was no need to waste time uncoupling the engine, running it back and coupling up again at the other end when due out; the driver simply had to walk back along the train.

Lance, however, was at first aghast at being in the cab on his own; he wasn't even a qualified fireman, he said.

"True," agreed George but he added, "don't you want a promotion one day?"

"Yeah, but cor! - on me own in the cab of a movin' train!"

"Just think, Lance, if you do this, it'll look very good on your file in the office. It shows a serious responsibility."

Lance smiled slowly. "Yeah, it does an' all!" He understood that the suggestion also clearly showed his driver had regained belief in his ability, and that he, Lance, had learned his lesson. He just hoped he could handle what was going to be a fairly tricky duty.

They travelled on the cushions to Wrexham to pick up their train; Lance eyed the front of the autocoach with its curious cab instead of a blank wall or a corridor connection. The front was spanned by three windows, and a large bell was fixed above them; this was to warn any gangers or other railwaymen on the track ahead as they might not hear the sound of the locomotive in the centre or the rear of the train.

The 7.34 Wrexham was an important train for the large number of Chester railway divisional staff, many of whom lived in Wrexham and were required to be in their offices by 8.30am every day. Welsh was commonly spoken in the train as the shoppers and railwaymen discussed the day's events and plans while travelling to and from Chester.

The auto train duty was a success, although it nearly came badly to grief on one occasion. The engine was a little 1400 class 0-4-2T tank engine which had a surprising turn of speed between its two coaches. Lance had been instructed as to the various codes he would hear from George at the front of the train and after the first two days he felt more comfortable on his own in the cab. Between Wrexham and Chester there were several stops to allow him to fill any gaps in the fire, although keeping up steam pressure on the short journey was not a challenging job in any case. In fact it almost led to a potentially embarrassing complacency; on one return trip with a light load back south, he had forgotten to check the steam pressure and nearly came to grief on the bank between Rossett and Gresford. He had to frantically shovel a light layer of coal over the firebed then open the dampers, then the firedoor, wide for maximum combustion, hoping the engine wouldn't stall. He later admitted his fault to George, who nodded; he had noticed the lack of power and had to open the regulator wide and keep his fingers crossed, wondering whether Lance would explain. Lance's honesty confirmed George's opinion of the lad's potential.

Lance felt proud of himself after successfully completing this duty and lost no time in informing his new girlfriend about his achievement. She was a prim and serious young woman, who made it clear that she liked a man with a strong sense of responsibility, and privately thought Lance could now conceivably earn himself an occasional chaste kiss.

"I was on me tod in the cab of a 40-tonne locomotive," he told her. She nodded in approval. "Nice to see that you can be trusted with such an important duty."

"Yeah, well, that's wot they think o' me in the Great Western," he boasted.

Other cleaners in the shed were equally pleased. "It'll be a real leg up for yer, Lance me lad," said one of them.

"Aye, it will an' all," agreed Lance, then added thoughtfully, "an' wot's more, it might 'elp get the knickers off me new bird!"

20 - The calm before the storm (November 1938)

The situation in Europe was beginning to look rather ugly. The Poles were unhappy about the threatening attitudes of their neighbours on both sides; the Russians and Germans. The French were unhappy about the Italian naval build-up in the Mediterranean, as were the British, who were equally unhappy with the growing strength of the German navy. Chamberlain, the British Prime Minister, was doing his best to keep the peace but was being harassed in and out of Parliament by some of his colleagues, particularly by Mr Winston Churchill, who was regarded by many as a warmonger. There were unsettling rumours of domestic activities on the part of the German government, which suggested that the Nazis were dealing with their own opposition rather more firmly than even Mosley's British Union of Fascists were entirely happy about. All in all, it was a worrying time for the British Establishment.

The general public, however, did not share these worries; life was looking rather better now that employment levels were beginning to improve, and people were more willing to part with their money than they had been a few years earlier. The summer had proved to be a very satisfactory holiday season for the GWR, which was preparing itself for what it hoped would be heavy summer holiday traffic the following year. The problem lay not so much north of Wolverhampton but rather in the west, where the build-up of summer Saturday traffic to the West Country could cause long delays to many trains. The route west of Bristol could not readily cope with the demands in summer, and holiday trains could easily be held up

147

for hours. The problem was seen to be so urgent that management was seriously investigating the possibility of electrifying the line west of Taunton. Detailed plans were being drawn up to ascertain what types of electric locomotive might be needed and of the relative costs in coal between steam and electric propulsion if the route were to be electrified.

The enginemen at Chester shed had received the new Swindon locomotive, the Grange class 4-6-0, with much appreciation; it was designed to be a more modern mixed traffic 4-6-0 Hall-type locomotive with smaller wheels. But in spite of the smaller wheels, it could still run when necessary and seemed to have a slight edge on the Hall for power and the improved boiler proved to be more forgiving to an inexperienced driver. Another new locomotive from Swindon was a smaller Manor class 4-6-0, but there were not many of these; they had been designed to replace the life-expired Mogul 2-6-0s, but Chester men hadn't seen any yet and were unable to comment on them, although worrying rumours about their steaming capacity had begun to circulate.

George had over the years a range of firemen to work with, most of them for relatively short periods of time, including at one time an Australian who George felt should have been thinking of taking his driver's exam. The man was a fine fireman, but he was missing his family and had resigned in order to catch a boat home. He said he thought war was coming and he wanted to be ready for the defence of his country.

"I can see us getting into a serious argument with the Germans," said one engineman in the enginemen's mess, "but why in hell would they want to attack Australia?"

"Yair, well while you Poms are keeping the Germans busy, Downunder the Japs'll be looking to cause strife, an' they'll be lookin' at us!"

George had read of the annoyance the Japanese government had felt with the Americans but, like most Britons, he didn't think that was anything the Americans couldn't handle; furthermore, in any case, the Japanese were too busy in China to take on any more enemies. But if the Japanese did try anything against the British Empire, surely the big naval bases in Singapore and Hong Kong could deal with them. No, in his view, the Germans were the ones to worry about and he wasn't sure the British and French armies were truly ready for any serious engagements.

"We've got great battleships which could easily sort out those Japs," replied the engineman, "then there's the Yanks – they'd help for sure. No, I wouldn't worry about the Japs, mate."

"P'raps not, but I'm still going back to Melbourne; there's a sheila there I'd like to catch up with, if she isn't already hitched."

There was general laughter around the cabin and nods of approval.

"What do you think, George?" asked one elderly driver, "you were in the Great War; would you be prepared to go back to fight the Germans if they attacked us?"

"I met a lot of German soldiers," said George, "and I'll tell you something you might not like to hear. Most of them were doing exactly what most of us were doing. They were fighting because their politicians ordered them to; the only difference was we won."

"Well what about the newspapers' reports about what they're doing to the Jews?"

George paused, then added, "I think that's a fairly recent business, and I agree that it's savage. But that's what we will get if Mosley and his thugs have anything to do with it."

As they were discussing the situation, another driver came in. "Guess what, lads; I've just come from a run from Wellington to Crewe and I've seen the latest engines the LMS have; they're magnificent! Bloody great streamlined Pacific 4-6-2s. All bright red with gold stripes along the sides. They've also got some non-streamlined jobs at Crewe North shed and they look very good, too. A driver there told me they could take sixteen on from Euston to Carlisle non-stop. We should never have let Stanier go to the LMS; he should have been kept with us."

"You're colourblind, Fred," said another driver, "when I saw one it was blue with silver stripes."

"You're both right," said George, "I was talking to the fireman on the Holyhead yesterday on Platform Four, and he explained that both colour schemes are used. He also said that he'd fired one and it was very hard work – the steam coal pusher wasn't as much help as they thought it would be."

"They should use Gresley's idea of a corridor in the tender so you can change crews on the run," commented Fred, adding as he stared across the cabin to a portly driver, "wouldn't suit you, Alf; no tender corridor would be wide enough to let you through!"

It wasn't only the LMS who were providing innovations; George and Alice were in London for a week, visiting friends who proudly showed them their new television set. It was a big cabinet with a tiny screen, rather like a miniature cinema, and they could watch up-to-date news and other interesting programmes on it.

Young Ben was fascinated. "Can we have one, Dad?"

"Sorry, Ben," replied his father, "firstly it's too expensive for us, and secondly we don't live here. The service only extends round London. You'll have to wait until the service has a wider spread and also, incidentally, until the GWR decides its enginemen are underpaid and award us a big wage increase. Can you see that happening in the present climate?" (The GWR had suffered major flooding in South Devon and two serious fires in signal boxes on the Paddington approaches, all of which required expensive repair work.)

Ben shook his head, "No, Dad."

"Neither can I."

But this didn't stop both families from avidly watching the television news every day of their visit.

On his return to duties, George decided it was time that his wife met Lance, who had become his regular fireman in spite of being still only a Passed Cleaner. George warned Alice that the lad was unsophisticated and that he had an openly lecherous nature, but that in spite of these things he was highly competent in his work and a very entertaining mate in the cab.

When Lance arrived, Alice was immediately impressed with his manners, as well as his obvious attempt to spruce himself up; she saw a personable young man with an open, honest manner - the sort of lad most girls would instinctively approve of at first sight. After a brief questioning of his home life, she asked him about a girlfriend.

"No, Mrs Denton," replied Lance, "I 'aven't got no bird fer meself, not reg'lar like. Some birds wear nice dresses wot turn yer on, but when yer turned on they won't let yer do anyfink. Gets right up me nose, that does."

Mrs Denton nodded sympathetically. "A fireman's life is terribly hard."

"Err- yeh," Lance frowned; he wasn't sure whether he was being teased.

George smiled quietly to himself; Alice, standing ladylike and poised, had done a good job of reacting with dignity to Lance's use of the street vernacular but he was privy to another side of her, where prudishness and manners were shed like clothes, in favour of honest passion.

Nevertheless, the evening was a success, but George was disappointed that their son Ben was not there to meet Lance; he would have enjoyed the experience. Alice, however, was pleased; Ben might have learned from Lance something that he was not ready for, in her view. It was fortunate, she felt, that he was away at Manchester University, starting his Economics course.

Just after the Christmas break, George and Lance were on a freight from Birkenhead docks to Wolverhampton where they would hand over their engine, an elderly Aberdare 2-6-0, still in reasonable condition, to an Oxley Crew. They would take the train further on to Birmingham and return the engine the following day. They had been asked to place a large, experimental tarpaulin over the cab to extend to the tender.

"To keep the rain off?" asked Lance of the fitter in the shed. "About bloody time too; you should try drivin' in the rain, like wot we 'ave ter."

The fitter grinned, "No mate; it's ter stop enemy airplanes from seein' yer fire at night and droppin' their bombs on yer 'ead!"

"Garn!" said Lance, "yer pullin' me leg!"

When George arrived and saw the tarpaulin, his eyes narrowed; Lance told him how the fitter had tried to tease him, but George did not smile.

"What's up, Mr D?" asked Lance uncertainly.

"They're Air Raid Precautions, Lance," replied George, "we didn't have much bombing in the Great War, but now things are different; there could be big, heavy aeroplanes with bigger bombs coming over. A light from below might help them. I've joined the ARP."

"Wot's that mean?"

"It means Air Raid Precautions; we go out at night and check that no lights are showing, from houses or engines, amongst other things."

Lance was silent; he couldn't imagine what it would be like to be involved in a serious armed conflict with another country.

Approaching the Black Country, as the area was known due to the smoke and bleak open landscape from the heavy industries, Lance stared as they passed some of the railway buildings. Windows were being taped and walls sandbagged, and some of the buildings were having their window areas bricked up.

"Broad sticky bands over windows, sandbagged walls, tarps over yer 'ead, Air Raid Precautions? What're we comin' to, Mr D?"

George sighed; he knew what life for the fighting soldier was really like, and wondered whether it would claim Ben's life; he was already in the Manchester University Territorial Army.

"Lance, my lad, the Great Western Railway is preparing for war."

Glossary

For those less familiar with a few of the terms used by railwaymen of the first half of the twentieth century.

Banker: Extra engine used at the back of a train to assist it uphill.

Bay platform: Platform with a buffer stop at one end.

Blow-back: Rare burst of fire into the cab.

Bobby: Signalman.

Bogies: Railway term for coaches. Also a set of four or six wheels in a frame.

Brake van: Small van at the end of a goods train from which the guard could apply a brake to assist the driver when slowing the train. In a passenger train, the brake van would be a coach with a section for the guard.

Bushes: The thicker metal areas around the holes through which the coupling and connecting rods were attached to the wheels.

Big ends: The wider ends of the tapered connecting rods where they were attached to the driving wheel; the narrow ends were attached to the shaft into the cylinder.

Cleaner: Apprentice engine cleaner preparing to become first a fireman then later a driver.

Clinker: Partly-burned coal remnants which would stick to the grate and needed to be removed to allow air through the fire to aid combustion.

Corridors: Railway term for coaches used in longer-distance trains.

They had corridors with toilets, as opposed to the non-corridor trains used for short distances.

Clear: A signal which indicates that the route ahead is clear for a train to proceed.

Control: The department of the railway company responsible for managing crewing of trains.

Detonators: Small explosive devices placed on the track to warn approaching trains in an emergency. On hearing detonators, a driver would stop immediately.

Distant signal: The signal giving warning of the status of the next section of track but one. Normally yellow with a black chevron stripe.

Down: The route direction away from London (see also 'Up').

Driver: The man responsible for driving the locomotive.

Empty Coaching Stock (ECS): A train of empty coaches to be taken where they were needed. These trains were not advertised in the public timetables and did not carry passengers.

Firebox: The section of the locomotive immediately in front of the cab, in which the fire would be situated.

Fireman: The man responsible for keeping the fire at a level sufficient to maintain enough steam for the driver to drive.

Fitted goods: A goods train fitted with vacuum brakes, which would allow it to travel at higher speeds than an unfitted goods.

Fouling point: The point in a siding at which a stabled train is clear of the main line.

Ganger: A member of a team whose job it was to check and maintain the safe condition of the railway trackwork.

Guard: The man in charge of a train. He travelled in the brake van at the rear of a goods train or passenger train.

Headshunt: Extra siding to allow a locomotive to wait before backing onto a train or to permit a shunting operation without interfering with station or yard approach tracks.

Home signal: The signal controlling the next section of track. Normally red with a white stripe.

Hot box: Hot axle box of a vehicle filled with grease or oil; if it got too hot it could start a fire.

Injector: Pump in a steam locomotive to force water into the boiler.

Knocker up: A cleaner who would be used to wake up enginemen when they were needed on shift.

Lay-by: A siding in which a slower train could wait while a faster train passed.

Light engine: An engine without a train.

Loose coupled: A train of goods vehicles fitted only with metal couplings and thus limited to a speed of 40 mph.

Loop: Side track to allow a train to be marshalled for departure or after arrival without blocking the main line.

Main: Tracks for fast trains.

Metals: Rails or tracks.

Non-corridors: Coaches used in short distance trains did not normally have their compartments connected by corridors.

Passed Cleaner/Fireman: Cleaner or fireman who had satisfied the authorities that he could be trained for promotion to the next rank. He could be used as a fireman/driver under training.

Pilot engine: Engine which would be added in front of a train engine and used to assist with a heavy train.

Plug: A fusible lead plug in the boiler which would melt if the water level sank too low, thus releasing steam pressure to prevent the boiler from exploding.

Regulator: Large lever in the cab of locomotives, enabling the driver to regulate the flow of steam to the cylinders, essentially controlling the speed of the train.

Semi-fast: Passenger train which does not stop at all stations.

Shed: Depot for steam locomotives. Locomotives were allotted to a particular shed which was responsible for their day-to-day maintenance.

Shedmaster: Foreman in charge of a shed.

Shocvan: Goods van with special springs to prevent damage during shunting.

Siding: Stretch of track used to store vehicles until they were required.

Single: 4-2-2 express passenger locomotive with a single large driving wheel on each side. It was designed by William Dean and many observers at the time believed it to be the most beautiful engine ever designed.

Signalling: Used to control the movement of trains. A 'home' signal controlled the entry to a section. If it showed 'clear', entry was permitted. If it showed 'danger', entry was not permitted.

A 'distant' signal warned of the position of the next home signal; a clear meant that the next home signal was also clear, whereas a danger meant that the next home signal showed danger also and that the driver should prepare to stop his train at the next signal.

Slow: Tracks for slow/stopping trains.

Sole and heel: Light maintenance and repair to a locomotive.

Special: Non-timetabled train for a special purpose.

Steam heating: Most passenger trains had their coaches heated by steam pipes throughout the train.

Steam lance: Hose which could be connected to the boiler of a locomotive to force superheated steam through the boiler tubes to clear them of any blockages.

Steam pressure: The pressure of steam in the locomotive boiler.

Stopper: Passenger train which stops at most or all stations on its route.

Tank engine: Locomotive incorporating a bunker for coal and tanks for water; used for short-distance work. As tank engines could travel either smokebox- or bunker-first they did not need to turn on a turntable.

Tender: Special vehicle attached behind a steam locomotive to carry the coal and water needed.

35-tonners: Railway term for coaches. 35 tonnes was the standard weight of most coaches.

Unfitted goods: Goods train in which the vehicles are not fitted with vacuum brakes. See also 'loose coupled'.

Up: The route direction towards London.

Water troughs: Long metal troughs filled with water between the rails to allow locomotives to pick up water at speed.

Wheel tapper: Metallurgy expert who tapped the wheels of vehicles with a special hammer to listen for metal fatigue.

Railway companies mentioned in the text

Before the Grouping of 1923 there were many private railway companies in Britain, each with their distinctive rolling stock and colours:

CLC = Cheshire Lines Committee

GCR = Great Central Railway

L&Y = Lancashire and Yorkshire Railway

LNWR = London and North Western Railway

LSWR = London and South Western Railway

MR = Midland Railway

S&DJR = Somerset and Dorset Joint Railway

The Grouping merged Britain's railways into four main companies:

GWR = Great Western Railway

LMS = London Midland and Scottish railway

LNER = London and North Eastern Railway

SR = Southern Railway

These companies were nationalised in 1948.

Acknowledgements

As in previous books in this series, I am heavily in debt to Katharine Smith of Heddon Publishing, for her constant encouragement and editorial input, which can only enhance any author's work. I have also been fortunate to be able to rely on the technical and stylistic expertise of Dr John Ritter, whose knowledge of steam locomotive working has added greatly to whatever success this book may have. The publishers are also grateful to the Great Western Trust for the use of the photograph on the front cover.

22351071R00103

Printed in Poland
by Amazon Fulfillment
Poland Sp. z o.o., Wrocław